FETISH

SENATE

FETISH

An account of unusual erotic desires

CLAVEL BRAND

SENATE

Fetish

Previously published in paperback in 1970 by
Riverhaven Ltd, London

This paperback edition published in 1997 by Senate,
an imprint of Random House UK Ltd, Random House,
20 Vauxhall Bridge Road, London SW1V 2SA.

Copyright © Riverhaven Ltd/Luxor Press Ltd 1970

ISBN 1 85958 500 0

Printed and bound in Great Britain by
Cox & Wyman, Reading, Berkshire

Contents

INTRODUCTION

VIRTUALLY anything can serve as a fetish. It is a common mistake to assume that a fetish must be intrinsically and obviously sexual, although, since we know that the chosen object serves as a sexual substitute, it is an understandable error. The sexual element is not necessarily contained by the fetish at all. A very large number of fetishes lack any discernible sexual properties but are endowed with them by the fetishist himself who projects his sexual longings, needs and feelings on to the object for a variety of reasons about which it is dangerous to generalize but which will emerge during the following discussion.

A fetish, as has been explained many times, was originally understood to be a magic charm, a sort of talisman which protected the wearer or even, in some instances, increased virility. In the currect sexological sense, of course, it means simply a substitute, something which stands in place of the orthodox sexual outlets. A fetish's relation to physical sexual expression obviously varies. It is not necessarily an end in itself but frequently acts as a stimulating agent or preliminary to a shared sexual performance. However, the importance of the fetish is such that arousal and orgasm are virtually impossible if the chosen substitute is removed.

Bearing this latter point in mind, it is possible to see that something of the original idea of the charm or talisman remains even in current, specific usage of the term.

This point is generally neglected in discussions of fetishism but an understanding of it does much to explain the complex relationship which inevitably exists between the fetishist and the fetish. Discussions of fetishism are necessarily objective and researchers are quick to point out that a fetish has a limiting and undesirable effect on the life of the fetishist. At the same time, most writers on the subject also admit that to the enslaved fetishist, the object is welcomed and viewed as a sort of sexual salvation. For all their apparent contradictoriness, both statements are true. One is objective, the other completely subjective, and in the latter we see important vestiges of the original meaning of the term. The fetishist is always sexually inadequate without the presence, be it tactile, visual, odoriferous or even aural, of the fetish. It is, in other words, his charm which protects him against the fears which prevent normal sexual expression, or which makes him potent. It is something to which his faith is pinned and is magic in the sense that it apparently makes possible the otherwise impossible. If we understand this we can grasp something of the tenacity with which the fetishist clings to his particular charm and why he has such difficulty in accepting the objective view that the fetish, rather than solving the initial and most important problem, only exacerbates it.

It has frequently been pointed out that we are all fetishists in one sense. The fixing of our affections, physical and emotional, on one partner is a form of fetishism which has been encouraged, particularly in the Western World, by both social and ecclesiastical forces. However, since such attraction does not interfere with natural sexual expression, nor exclude the possibility of our having sexual relations with other partners, it does not fall under the scrutiny of clinical examination. Also, of course, such 'fetishistic' relationships are deemed to be preferable, in moral and social terms, to an indiscriminate sharing of sexuality. Therefore, a fetish, in clinical terms, is something which stands in place of the chosen partner. It is, broadly speaking, a love affair between a person and an object, and not two people.

But in spite of the fact that anything can gain the sexual attention of the fetishist, it is possible and useful to recognise that there are three main categories of objects which attract the fetishistically inclined. It would undoubtedly be possible to fill a book with exceptional and almost unprecedented examples of fetishistic involvement, but such cases are most usefully considered in relationship to the major groups. In the ensuing discussion we have attempted a compromise by considering the main groups separately but basing our choice of examples on some of the more unusual forms of fetish involvement which come under the main headings.

These headings are Clothing, Material, and Natural, or Bodily, Fetishism. In a subject as various and complex as this there is necessarily some overlapping from one group to another, but not to such an extent that the groups cannot be regarded as independent for the purposes of discussion. There is an obvious connection, of course, between shoe and foot fetishism, yet so exclusive and loyal is the fetishist to his preferred object that it is common for a shoe fetishist to have no interest whatsoever in the foot that wears the shoe and *vice versa*. These overlapping areas, however, will be indicated and discussed where relevant.

The basic attraction of clothing fetishism is obvious since the connection between the body, i.e. the natural sexual object, and that which covers it is self-evident. Clothing fetishism is also the largest of the three groups, for reasons

9

that will be explored later. The second largest is material fetishism, by which we mean the attraction felt by some people towards the fabrics with which clothes are made, i.e. silk, nylon, leather, etc. We can see at once that this particular fetishism is at one remove from clothing fetishism. There is an obvious connection between the two but material fetishism is less specific and can include materials which are not normally used for the manufacture of clothing, e.g. rubber. Even so, materials have their own specific attractions and it is possible to cite many examples in which the way in which the material is made up is quite unimportant to the fetishist. It is, in fact, the intrinsic qualities of the material which attract and this makes it necessary for us to regard this form of fetishism as separate and independent of clothing. The third and final group is also the smallest and is more commonly designated partial fetishism. We call it 'natural' because it is concerned with parts of the agreed natural sexual object, i.e. the human body. Foot fetishism would obviously fall into this category, but it should be understood that the chosen part, the foot, breasts, hair or whatever, is the main and even the sole source of attraction. The rest of the body is unimportant, as are the objects and materials which normally cover it.

We have also included a brief examination of what may be regarded as an offshoot of natural fetishism. This is defect or injury fetishism, a rather neglected area of the subject which is especially interesting since it tends to deviate from the normal pattern of fetishism in a number of small but crucial details. It comes under the main heading of natural fetishism because it, too, is concerned with parts of the human body, with the difference that the chosen part must be in some way deformed or damaged. Thus the

10

equivalent of the foot fetishist is the man who is attracted and aroused by a club foot. In such cases the whole, or healthy, body does not in any way attract the defect fetishist.

It would seem logical for the size of the three groups to be otherwise. Natural fetishism, simply because it is most closely allied to the human body, would logically be the largest, then clothing and finally material. But this is not so, obviously because fetishism is not intrinsically logical and because the majority of fetishists, who might also be regarded as the most acute examples, require to be distanced from the body or obvious sexual object. The fetishist's initial failure is to accept the human body as his or her sexual object. Therefore it is easier to accept a substitute which is distanced from the body as a whole. There are, however, other reasons which we shall discuss in due course.

The biggest problem faced by the layman trying to comprehend the power of fetishism is to understand how an inanimate object or non-sexual part of the body can be preferred to the body and mind of a total human being. Firstly, it must be understood that the beautiful woman who seems desirable to the average man does not attract the fetishist; not necessarily because he is unable to appraise and appreciate her charms, but because he feels himself inadequate to serve her for various reasons. It is within the grasp of anyone to understand the trauma experienced by the man who, faced with a willing and desirable woman, is unable to get and maintain an erection. What was desirable then becomes fearful and this fear only increases his failure. But his desire for a sexual outlet does not diminish and he naturally seeks an alternative. Secondly, it helps if one regards the fetish as a sexual symbol in the true sense of the phrase. A beautiful woman's desirability is increased by the man's mental knowledge of what he can do with her. Similarly, the fetishist experiences the woman via the object. He may in fact be making love to a piece of velvet, or a pair of pants, but these objects are connected in his mind with the ideal partner. Their advantage, as far as he is concerned, is that they are inanimate and absolutely controllable. They cannot observe, comment upon and broadcast his failure as a woman can. They make him feel safe and since the human sexual mechanism is so delicately balanced it is essential that all inhibiting tensions and fears be stilled if sexual expression is to be achieved.

This, then, is the predicament of the fetishist. His natural means of sexual expression is blocked and he seeks some comfortable substitute on which to project his often exaggerated (as a direct result of frustration) desire. How he does so and why are the subjects we will now begin to explore.

PART ONE: CLOTHING FETISHISM

1: The Problem of Sexual Focus

NUDITY is natural. We are born naked and unlike animals we do not later grow a concealing covering of fur to protect us. When we are completely unclothed we are in our natural state. It is, perhaps, a great pity that Nature did not endow us with some natural fleece. We are, certainly, the most vulnerable of beings as a result of our unprotected nakedness but that is of slight importance compared with the subtle problems which have arisen as a result of our wholesale adoption of clothing. Being naked we are vulnerable to cold and to damage from the natural world. It was in an attempt to counteract these grave disadvantages that man first began to cover himself, to imitate the animals by borrowing their pelts. The ability to reason, which forms the basis of our superiority over the animal kingdom, magnificent as it is, is little protection from wind or rain and cannot shield us from thorns and stones when we have no choice but to penetrate the forest or climb the mountain. Clothing, therefore, became essential. Without it we were ill-equipped as a species to survive.

Had clothing become no more than an essential protection against a harsh world there would be no problem. But four disparate factors combined to influence the development of clothing so that the natural human reactions to the body were displaced. Once man had discovered the advantages of clothing he also discovered that certain parts of his body required more protection and, even more significantly, that he himself wanted to preserve certain regions from danger. To cover himself from head to toe was impractical for a man whose survival depended upon his ability to move swiftly and untrammelled. He quickly discovered that his arms and legs, the most important parts of his body on a hunting expedition, could withstand a fairly high degree of rough treatment. But his stomach and genitals could not, and since the latter were the source of both perpetuation and great pleasure, he protected them. Similarly, women discovered that their breasts were extremely vulnerable and possessed a low pain threshold, as well as hampering them in manual work. Hence they were bound and protected. The female genitals, however, because of their placement, are naturally well protected, and it seems probable, therefore, that they were covered in imitation of men. Those parts of the body which had been unremarkably on display were now covered, for essentially practical reasons.

The second factor which affected the development of clothing among human beings lends force to the immemorial idea of woman as the instigator of man's downfall. The Eve in women prompted them to regard and develop clothing as a form of bodily adornment. Clothes were made beautiful to set off the woman's natural beauty, or to attract attention to a plain woman. And not content with adorning herself she made her man attractive as well. Once established this concern with adornment can be traced throughout the historical development of clothing and, because the first rude garments covered the genitals and specifically sexual regions of the body, adornment has inevitably centred upon these areas. The best and most obvious example is, of course, the codpiece which exaggerated and drew attention to the male crotch. Women responded by pushing forward the breasts and by adopting bright colours. It is a process which in our own time has taken on a new lease of life with the sudden upsurge in colourful and erotic fashions.

The third factor is a symptom of man's innate curiosity. It is his will to know, to reduce everything to a comprehensible explanation, which has been the motive cause of his extraordinary development. But it has also engendered problems which are not at all necessary. It is a basic impulse of human beings to find that which is concealed exaggeratedly attractive. It is not for nothing that we habitually talk of the veils of mystery. When something is masked from open view it teases man's mind, fires his imagination and lends the concealed object a false but powerful glamour. When we consider that the sexual parts of the body were not only concealed but adorned so that they became, as it were, more attractive by proxy we can see that the development of clothing created an explosive sexual situation.

The fourth and final factor which influenced our attitudes to clothing was the development of the predominantly Western concept of modesty. Concealment of the body, and especially of the genitals and female breasts, became a virtue. Natural nudity was pronounced sinful and wrong. By covering the body the Church decided that we lessened the possibility of physical temptation. An embargo was placed on sex and by hiding the body it was thought to frustrate the passions. This had two results. Those who admitted and enjoyed their sexual desires used clothing to heighten their attractiveness. They discovered that it was possible to stay covered and yet fix the attention by adornment and carefully controlled semi-exposure on the sexual potential of the body. The laws of propriety were thus observed, if somewhat liberally interpreted. But from the point of view of our subject, by far the most devastating effect of this idea of modesty and chastity was to fix, particularly the male, attention on the clothes themselves. Man's desire flourished, despite the prohibitions of Church and State, and he soon discovered that if he might not examine the body, he could enjoy its covering. The very objects of concealment, therefore, became symbols of that which was concealed. The Christian propagation of bodily modesty, and man's natural curiosity about anything that is concealed, served to refocus sexual attention on clothing which, as the fetishist undoubtedly proves, can be more erotic than any nudity.

Thus nudity was forbidden. The natural became unnatural and *vice versa*. When nudity was commonplace, as is borne out today by nudist colonies throughout the world and by unsophisticated tribes, sex occupied its proper role in life. When a group of people are habitually nude they quickly learn to accept the bodies of others. All the men do not go around in a state of perpetual erection, nor do the women long to throw themselves down on their backs. There is a time and a place for sex which is not altered or in any way heightened by perpetual nudity. Human beings seem to find a sort of relaxed courage from the certainty that sex, or food, etc., are available to them at any time. But once even only apparent barriers are erected between them and their needs, they display all the symptoms of frustration. Clothes are one such barrier and their effect has been to create a preoccupation with sex simply because the natural visual and tactile appetites have been frustrated. Far from inculcating a respect for modesty, clothes have exaggerated the sexual concern.

16

Thus man became used to clothing and not to nudity. It soon became commonplace for people to reach sexual maturity and even adulthood without having any idea of what the opposite sex looked like unclothed. All they had to to go on, all anyone had to go on, were the confusing and highly erotic hints provided by clothing. This, naturally, fired the imagination, with the result that the nude body became an ideal and the removal of clothing a sort of symbolic rape. It must be admitted, of course, that clothing can also be said to have provided an added spice to the whole business of eroticism, but its disadvantages far outweight such niceties of sophistication in the final analysis. This whole process, of course, often meant that the body itself was a disappointment when it was finally revealed. Nothing ever quite lives up to the imagined ideal. Some people find it difficult to see anything particularly attractive in the nude body, which fashion has frequently forced into an idealized shape which bears scant resemblance to the true form. Indeed it may be said that almost everything about clothing conspired to present a false sensuality which fed the imagination and increased frustration.

This is, in fact, what we mean by the problem of sexual focus. In a natural world, the genitals and the female breasts are the natural focus for the sexual imagination. If these areas are openly displayed then they are properly associated with their true function and there is no mystery, no room for speculation, except, of course, for that mystery which always surrounds the sexual act. But everything is clearly defined. The libido is properly directed. But clothing shifted the sexual focus on to itself and fashion created, at various times, new focuses. If a woman was covered from head to toe in thick material, but her arms were left bare, this had the effect of dramatizing, by contrast, her natural flesh. Thus what is exposed takes on an unnatural attraction. Bustles deliberately fixed the erotic eye on the buttocks, just as the codpiece dramatized the natural masculine bulge. When skirts were long and voluminous, the contrast provided by a glimpse of ankle was quite out of proportion to its true merit. By allowing women in particular to expose the so-called 'innocent' areas of the body clothing redirected sexual focus in a way which, it will be obvious, provided a breeding ground for fetishism. Dainty feet protruding under long, blanket-like skirts, or bare hands from tight sleeves, are obviously given a false attraction simply because they appear shockingly accessible by contrast with the rest of the body. The plunging neckline is, of course, an obvious and definitive example.

Thus in a sense we may say that fetishism, at least as far as clothing is concerned, has been deliberately encouraged as a result of this shifting of sexual focus. Such is the power of human beings and the strength of their abiding interest in sex that even a sackcloth shroud can be made attractive by a little adornment and a few cunningly placed tears. Indeed, we should be grateful that in view of this systematic frustration and perversion of natural attitudes such a low percentage of human beings have become fetishists. In the vast majority of cases there is, happily, no ultimate substitute for the human body and when this happens we can afford to regard clothing as a spice-providing, interest-catching sexual adornment. But for those who have been conditioned and prepared for fetishistic slavery by the unnatural emphasis that civilization has placed on clothing, it is not possible to take such a light-hearted view. They are the victims of clothing, men and women who have been, through no fault of their own, so susceptible to the eroticism of clothing that the naked body comes as a shock or a disappointment. It is inevitable that such people should reject the nude body and turn instead to its ambivalent coverings. We have, in fact, until very recent times, turned nudity into a bogy with which to frighten people into an adherence to laws which, no matter how socially desirable, are fundamentally unnatural. The most natural thing in the world, the common denominator between all people, the naked body, has for centuries been condemned and confined, but no such bridle could be fashioned for the imagination and human desires, with the result that many people have been led into a false focusing of sexual attention which has condemned them to a pernicious form of sexual enslavement which has blighted their lives.

It is seldom realized that the moment we invented clothing we also invented the possibility of striptease – a word which in itself sums up the frustrations clothing has inculcated – which, of course, sorts oddly with the idea of modesty. It has been stated many, many times that a partially clothed body is more erotic than a totally nude one. This idea has often been dismissed because it has been regarded as a last-ditch stand of the repressive factions who sought to cover the body at any price. But it is, in fact, very true, and it is a statement which has grave repercussions. If we compare, say, a photograph of a girl nude but for a pair of slinky black pants which she seems to be in the act of removing with one of a totally nude girl whose vagina is fully displayed, it is a proven fact that most men will find the partially clothed image more erotic, more exciting, than the nude one. This is an active demonstration of the power of concealment. But there are other factors which also influence and encourage this apparently illogical reaction. The moment man behaves in a flagrantly sexual way he is accused of being an animal. But what distinguishes him from the animals is his ability to reason and imagine. Therefore, since his body is not autonomous, he is most stimulated by that which permits him to exercise his imagination. The girl removing her pants does exactly that. No one can say precisely what he imagines will be revealed when the garment is removed, but it will certainly be something more exotic than the reality. But a naked girl displaying her most secret possession is stripped of all mystery. There is nothing left to the imagination. Total nudity, the display of the genitals, is comparable to an immediate climax. The end has been reached, the last veil stripped away before anything has really begun. Eroticism is replaced by animal sexuality which, because of the unique way in which he is constructed, is not nearly as satisfying or enjoyable to a man whose mind works in association with his body.

The point is that in its anxiety to forbid nudity and the frank enjoyment of the human body mankind has exaggerated this natural mutual process by propagating the wearing of clothes. We have forced ourselves to exercise our imagination by putting a barrier of fabric over our bodies and consequently we have turned the body into a mysterious, forbidden temple instead of accepting it as a natural condition of human life. We have developed a basically specious, fevered eroticism, which is full of many damaging pitfalls, instead of accepting a perfectly ordinary state. And when, as is inevitable, some people become exclusively focused on the trappings rather than the body, we condemn them as deviates and perverts.

Virtually everyone finds the act of undressing stimulating and, fortunately, the majority regard the final revelation of complete nudity the true end of the process. But some do not. For some, the sight of a semi-clothed person is much more exciting than a nude one. The naked body is an anti-climax when it is robbed of the mystery and tension engendered by a lace brassière, silk pants and long suspenders which combine to dramatize by contrast the appearance of the flesh. Nakedness can often be boring, the unclothed deeply exciting. The implications of this point to fetishism are patently obvious. In short, we have created opportunities for the fetishist to fix his sexual focus on ready-made substitutes. Clothes have, on many occasions, acted as a true barrier, cutting the fetishist off from true sexual fulfilment.

This general attitude has, of course, imbued our entire sexual outlook for centuries. We have repressed and forbidden, clothed and concealed, in the name of common good and spiritual excellence. In fact, all we have achieved is to cover all aspects of sex with a patina of forbidden glamour. We have manufactured a mystery out of a natural function. We have directly, though not intentionally, exploited man's curiosity. We have forced him into a position whereby what should be taken for granted has become a fatal fascination. It is ironic, therefore, that those who most deplore the human race's obsession with sex are those who are most determined to perpetuate this dark glamour which is the true cause of the obsession. Sadly, the whole process has now become universally accepted and even modern permissiveness is not able to tear down all the unnecessary veils. People today who advocate a return to the natural attitudes towards sex are surprised to find how quickly the attractions of nudity, for example, pall. The mystery is easily destroyed, but we are so conditioned to it that reality seems tame and even dull in comparison. We like and even treasure the *idea* of nudity, of naked sexual freedom, but we prefer to keep it as an ultimate goal and to go on paying lip-service to the deeply erotic concept of concealment and teasing, piecemeal revelation.

The clothing fetishist is the victim and the example of this process at its worst. The fetishist is the person who, for various reasons, or associations of reasons, makes do with a false sexual focus, who becomes fixed upon a substitute. Most of us are able to transcend the barriers we have erected. Most people can make the leap from concealment to nudity without hesitation. They are able to maintain a sense of perspective. No matter how much they may enjoy the eroticism of concealment, for them the final revelation of nudity is the climax which is expressed and realized by sexual intercourse. But for those who cannot do this clothing provides a ready substitute. Their sexual focus becomes fixed on some article of clothing which symbolizes the partner and acts as their charm against failure.

2: Underwear

FROM the fetishistic point of view by far the most important and dramatic development in the history of clothing was the introduction of underwear. Of all forms of clothing fetishism that which focuses the sexual attention on undergarments is the most common. Here, as throughout the rest of this discussion, our remarks will be mainly about women's clothing, for very few women are fetishists and their reactions tend to parallel those of the main body of fetishists who are, of course, men. The introduction of ladies' drawers or pants, and much later of the brassiere, added a new mystery to the female form. They assumed the role of the ultimate veil, which is always the most exciting, and since these garments were normally concealed from view, they took on an even greater air of mystery. Because they were essentially private garments a glimpse of them was as erotic as true nudity, or even more so since they left room for the exercise of the erotic imagination. When a woman is stripped to her underwear, she is generally considered to appear at her most erotic. Underwear does not conceal or alter the curves and planes of the human body but clings to and emphasizes the natural shape. Yet it conceals the detail. The erotic imagination receives a teasing stimulus. So much is revealed, yet these delightful, final details remain hidden. There is room for the mind to ponder and imagine.

Underwear provides an obvious sexual focus because its essential purpose is to cover the sexual parts of the body. A pair of lacy pants, for example, can never be divorced from their sexual connotations. They are designed and intended to be worn over the vagina and buttocks, and so they make an ideal sexual symbol for the fetishist. Furthermore, the excitement value of such garments is enhanced by their 'forbidden' nature. They are concealed. A woman does not normally show herself in her pants and brassiere and so there is an element of intrusion, of adventure, for the man who is attracted to them. With the adoption of short skirts, of course, pants became more accessible and were generally regarded as the last barrier between the male and the satisfaction of his desires. According to the code of seduction, once a man had got his hand beneath a woman's skirt there was very little to prevent him achieving at least a minor form of sexual release. Pants, then, and to a lesser extent the brassiere, became a centre of sexual focus, stood in place of the vagina and breasts. In this connection it is interesting to note that with the adoption of the miniskirt, female underwear has undergone a subtle change. For the young, who have virtually grown up in the presence of this revealing garment, which inevitably affords frequent glimpses of the wearer's underpants, this garment has lost much of its erotic allure through familiarity. For older men, however, it is a source of great stimulation because they have grown up in a world which took great pains to conceal underwear. However, the miniskirt has also resulted in the universal adoption of tights, which a great number of men have been quick to condemn. This all-enveloping garment greatly increases a woman's inaccessibility. They are virtually impenetrable, a fact which not only increases masculine frustration but which also demonstrates the fundamentally teasing nature of clothing. In a miniskirt a girl reveals more than ever, yet is considerably less accessible than when skirts were worn to the ankle and were voluminous. Significantly there is no indication at all that tights have become fetish objects for men. This is obviously partly because they are unattractive garments but also because their barrier-like qualities rob them of true eroticism. Furthermore it is probably not without significance that tights were, until very recently, an exclusively masculine garment. Their historical and archetypal connotations are of the male sex and not the female. All these factors combine to de-eroticize the garment which has now largely replaced pants as the closest to the female genitals. However, pants remain supreme both in terms of general eroticism and of fetishistic interest, and it seems highly unlikely that anything will replace them.

24

The symbolic power of female underwear is greatly enhanced by two things, their appearance and the materials from which they are made. Female underwear is a prime example of the feminine *penchant* for adornment. Frills, patterns, and delicate lace are all employed in the manufacture of underwear and these things have taken on a specifically feminine aura. Such frivolous prettiness seems to symbolize the essentially feminine attributes, just as the fine materials, silk, nylon, lawn, etc., imitate the softness and delicacy of a woman's skin. These are important factors to the fetishist, many of whom deplore the current predominance of functional feminine underwear. Man-made fibres, basic colours and a simplification of adornment are more practical for the busy modern girl and undoubtedly some of the glamour has been taken out of female underwear in recent years. Yet even the simplest pants are preferable to the sexless tights.

On the other hand it is extremely interesting to note that a parallel process of prettification has taken place in male underwear. The one-time completely functional male underpants have become briefer and more colourful. Indeed, they are often indistinguishable from the basic conception of female underwear. As a result, women are much more conscious of what men wear beneath their trousers and there has been a sudden upsurge of fetishistic interest in male underwear on the part of homosexual men. This seems to indicate that the actual appearance of underwear plays an important role in its adoption as a fetish object.

The extraordinary power exercised over the fetishist by female underwear is exemplified by Frederick C. Most of this mild man's week-ends are devoted to the pursuit of his obsession. He goes for long walks, oblivious of his surroundings except for glimpses of his desired sexual object.

He displays enormous patience in loitering at bus stops, watching for women who, as they mount the bus, reveal the line of their underpants beneath their tight skirts. Escalators and tube trains are full of opportunities for Frederick C to glimpse a girl's panties beneath her miniskirt. When his patience is rewarded he experiences a shortness of breath, his heart thumps and he feels all the sensations of arousal in his genitals. He will stand for as long as he possibly can outside a lingerie shop, literally devouring with his eyes the colourful display of dainty pants. At such times he gains an erection. He visits large department stores specifically in order to look at, and even handle, displays of women's pants. At sale times, when the big stores frequently put out trays of pants on display, he will linger as long as he dare, feeling the fine stuffs and examining the cut of all sorts of undergarments. Throughout this procedure he is fully aroused.

So conscious is he of his obsession that he will happily devote a day to the visual and tactile satisfaction of his desire, but he can never bring himself to buy any of the goods he so much admires. He feels too embarrassed and thinks that to actually purchase a pair of women's pants would be to give himself away. Yet he has three times been charged with stealing underwear from clothes lines. On many other occasions, he has gone undetected.

'The first time was quite unplanned. I'd spent the whole day looking for glimpses of women's pants, but had had no luck. It was almost dark and I was on my way home. I was on top of a bus and I was suddenly transfixed by a glimpse of a row of washing in a back garden. There were five pairs of pants, red, blue, black, all colours. I was so excited I couldn't stop trembling. I jumped off the bus at the next traffic lights and went back to the house. I must have walked up and down that road a hundred times just looking and growing more and more excited. I thought about the girl who must have worn them, and that only excited me more. At last I couldn't bear it any longer. I let myself into the garden and took the lot. I nearly had an orgasm as I pulled them from the line and then, of course, I was panic-stricken. I ran as fast as I could and got on the first bus that came along. My pockets were stuffed full of lacy nylon pants. I sat on the bus fingering them and had an erection all the time. Anyone who saw me must have thought I was mad. I was trembling, couldn't breathe properly. I was so excited I could hardly sit still. That's why I go on doing it, even though I know I shouldn't. The excitement is better than anything I've ever known. Nothing else can replace it and so I give way every so often and help myself to some more.'

With a pocketful of stolen pants, Frederick C evinces all the symptoms of a man suddenly presented with a desirable and available woman. But he has never had intercourse in his life. What, then, does he do with his booty?

'When I got home, I left the pants in my pocket. I knew that if I got them out straight away I would not have been able to contain myself. I stripped first, then I took the pants out and laid them on my bed. I had an orgasm at once, without even touching myself. But I still felt very sexy. I must have had three or four orgasms that night. I spent hours lying on my bed, handling and looking at the pants. When I was very excited, I would just tickle my erection by moving them gently up and down the length of my penis and along my perineum. Just the touch of the cold, silky nylon on my aroused flesh is sufficient to give me a shattering climax.

'At last, I was completely drained and then the full

27

enormity of what I had done hit me. I felt sick, not with shame, I liked my pants too much for that, but with fear. I had to get rid of them. I destroyed them, cut them with scissors and deposited the pieces in a waste bin on the other side of London. For a while after that I was O.K., but a month or so later I had to do it all over again. The third time, I got caught. And so it goes on.'

As far as it is possible to discover, Frederick C does not indulge in erotic fantasies during these fetishistic sessions. The mere feel and sight of the pants is sufficient to excite him. Their symbolic value, in his case, is such that there is no need for added stimulation. The destruction of the pants (he never retains any for more than a few hours) is a symbolic attempt to break the hold the fetish has on him. It is also a form of self-punishment. He feels very sad at the destruction of something he virtually loves, but this tearing and cutting somehow exonerates him from the guilt he feels for his theft and for having indulged himself.

Underwear fetishists often destroy the garments they prize, but for much more disturbing motives than Frederick C. John H, for example, both steals and buys women's pants, but he puts them to a different use. He masturbates himself and deliberately ejaculates over the pants. He does this several times and then destroys them. The act of destruction excites him enormously and he frequently ejaculates without manipulation while doing so. This is an act of symbolic sadism. By ejaculating on the garments he is 'dirtying' the female image. By destroying them he is wreaking his revenge on women who, he feels, have rejected him. This is the only way in which he can exercise masculine power over the female sex, as symbolized by underwear.

But to return to Frederick C. As we have said, he has

28

never experienced intercourse and his sole sexual outlet, the only form of sex which now interests him, is that which he has described in his own words. His is a fairly classic case, as these incidents from his youth reveal.

'I had no idea what girls were like physically until I was twenty-three. Not really, I mean. I began masturbating at about fourteen, after having had a series of wet dreams. It just seemed natural and I soon gathered that other boys did it. The first time I became really aware of a woman as a sexual creature was when I was fifteen. My mother used to do a bit of dressmaking for pin-money and one after-noon I was in the room while she fitted a young woman. She changed in the bedroom, but came back into the living-room when she'd got the dress on. I was lying on the floor. I think I'd been reading a book or something. This dress had a flared skirt and the woman stood, quite uncon-sciously, where I could see right up her skirt. She didn't have a slip on and for the first time in my life I saw a woman's pants. I lay there, looking up her long, beautiful legs. She had pink suspenders which disappeared under-neath her pants. They were white silk and I can clearly remember the way they hugged her bottom and showed off its shape. Around the legs was a deep froth of frilly lace. I got an erection at once. She stood talking to my mother for a long time and throughout I was staring and growing more and more excited. When she went back into the bed-room to change, I went to the bathroom and masturbated. Thereafter, I always conjured up the picture of her in her white, lace-trimmed panties whenever I masturbated.

'As I got older, I went out with several girls, but I was very timid and shy. I'd been very strictly brought up and very sheltered. I didn't know even then what men and women did together, so I never used to do more than kiss

29

a girl. But, slowly, I learned from the other lads at work and my friends. Of course the idea excited me but I was still too timid to really do anything. A girl only had to say "stop" or push my exploring hand away and I gave up. Then I heard about a girl at work who was supposed to be easy. Two of the boys I knew gave graphic details of what they had done with her. At last I plucked up the courage to ask her out and I was determined to go the whole way with her. I was twenty-three. Well, she was as willing as my informants had led me to believe. For the first time I had my hand on a girl's pants. The silky feel of them thrilled me. I was hard and trembling with excitement. I pushed up her skirt and saw her pants. They were pale blue with little embroidered flowers on the sides. I touched them, ran my hands all over them. Surreptitiously, I took out my penis and lay on top of her. The moment my hot flesh touched the cool silk of her pants I ejaculated. She was absolutely furious. Of course, I understand now how frustrated she must have been. I'd not done anything to arouse her really, and I'd stained her pants as well. But I didn't understand any of this at the time. She wanted me to try again and began to play with me, but she had taken off her pants and I just wasn't interested. I saw a naked girl for the first time and it did nothing for me at all. She made me use my hand on her eventually, but I was hopeless and hated it. She was angry and said I was a dead loss. She told the other boys about it at work and I had to leave. I've never even tried to go with a woman since.'

An adolescent's first awareness of a sexual object is crucial and frequently dictates the pattern of his future sexual development. In this case, the intensity of the over-protected, ill-informed Frederick C's excitement at the sight of the woman's white pants fixed this garment as the object

30

of sexual arousal. Being ignorant of female anatomy, the usually hidden pants acted as an involuntary sexual substitute. His later experience with the girl he worked with fixed this reaction finally. His inexperience prevented him from having proper control over his responses. His excitement was so acute at being able to view again the initial source of sexual arousal, of realizing his masturbatory fantasies, that it was not at all surprising that he should ejaculate prematurely. In the aftermath of sexual release, the girl's nudity seemed an anticlimax and her superior knowledge only increased his initial timidity. He conceived a dislike of the female body because he saw it at the wrong time. Had he seen the girl before ejaculating, he would probably have had a different reaction. But her scorn and anger wounded him. The mockery of his male colleagues when they heard the story can easily be imagined and would only have increased his sense of failure. He therefore fixed upon underwear as his sexual object rather than risk exposing himself again to his own inadequacies and the subsequent feminine scorn. With a different, more understanding girl, he may well have overcome his dislike of the female body, which is, in any case, only a symptom of his fear. But he has never tried. His sexual focus has remained fixed on underwear and women as such make no impact upon him, except as the wearers of sexually exciting pants.

Frederick C's case displays the most common way in which the fetishist discovers and becomes fixed upon the substitute. However, there are many other ways. A few years ago a great deal of publicity was given to the widespread, and originally American, practice of organized pantie-raids. This was a feature of American college co-education and consisted of the raiding of the girls' dormitories by a group of male students, each of whom returned carrying a pair of pants as a trophy. This phenomenon, which seems to have taken its place as part of the student ritual of America, was variously condemned as an example of youthful licentiousness or wrily regarded as an unremarkable manifestation of youthful high spirits. The latter was probably the saner view, for the panties were invariably handed over by the girls, or snatched from a drawer. However, it is unrealistic to pretend that this ritual did not possess fetishistic, as well as more commonplace sexual, overtones. There can be no doubt that this practice shows how universal is the attitude to feminine underwear as a sexual symbol. But this practice did lead to a fetishistic involvement for one young man, Bart V.

'I was a student at a small co-educational college in up-state New York during the early fifties. Pantie-raids were big news then and every self-respecting college and fraternity had to have them. My college was no exception and late one evening the whole of my fraternity raided the main girls' dormitory. It was a very innocent thing. I mean, no guy tore the pants off a girl or anything like that. Most of us had steady girl-friends in the dorm and they just handed over a pair. Other guys grabbed them off chairs or out of closets, and we all raced back to the frat house with our loot.

'I was dating a cute girl at the time who willingly handed me a wisp of pink nylon, all ruched and sheered, with little rosebuds set in the frills. Really pretty, feminine things. Anyway, we all high-tailed it back to the frat house, like I said, and compared our trophies. We'd got a few packs of canned beer back there, strictly against the college regulations, but we celebrated the deed by guzzling a few cans apiece.

32

'I guess we got pretty high – it didn't take much in those days – and some joker said we should put on our girl's pants and make 'em reclaim 'em the next day. In other words, the girls would have to strip 'em off us if they wanted their frillies back. Well, the idea appealed. It sort of opened up a lot of very interesting possibilities to a bunch of college kids. So, we all pledged to do it and peeled down our pants and shorts and put on the panties we had gotten from the girls.

'It was like nothing I'd ever known. I knew the minute I pulled that sheer nylon up my thighs that I'd discovered something wild. I got a charge that was out of this world. I had an erection at once, and got plenty of kidding about it from the other guys. Well, I shot my load in those pants and I slept in 'em. They turned me on better than any girl. All next day I was conscious of that cool, frilly stuff on my ass and crotch. But really, it felt so great, I was hard all day long. And if I thought of the girl who had been wearing them, thought about that stuff pressing against what she'd got down there, I really went wild.

'Well, my girl never got her pants back. She didn't try too hard and I just wanted to keep them. I've worn girls' panties ever since when I go on a date and I keep 'em on while I'm making love. I have to. Without them it's hopeless. Sometimes, when I've been wearing my own shorts I just can't get worked up at all, but let me wear a pair of lacy, delicate, frilly pants and man, there's no holding me.'

Bart V's fetishism was very quickly developed and its true genesis is veiled in mystery. It is, too, a mild form of fetishism, for he is still able to make the transference from fetish object to a woman. But it *is* a fetish, for his potency depends upon contact with feminine underwear. His pecu-

33

liar predilection has much in common with transvestitism but it would be wrong to call Bart V a transvestite. Even so, there must be some element of identification in his wearing feminine underclothing when he is with a woman. His response is primarily tactile. He consciously enjoys the sensation of the garment against his skin. This, in turn, makes him more conscious of his masculinity. Presumably this symbolic identification with the female partner fulfils some deep-seated need in him which failed to come to light in discussion of his problem. His is, however, an interesting example of the fetish as a magic charm. His virility is ensured by and dependent upon his wearing feminine pants and the method of discovering this need is most unusual. Furthermore, the fact that prior to the pantie-raid Bart V had always been normally potent with a girl shows that the fetish is, to a certain extent, chosen and that its effect is primarily psychological.

Another most unusual, but extremely revealing, case concerns a homosexual man in his late twenties who, of course, has a fetishistic fixation on male underpants. Paul R looks much younger than his age and completely lacks the flamboyance commonly evinced by homosexuals of the passive kind. Like so many fetishists he is timid and shy. Although he admits that he is a homosexual he has only ever had three shared encounters, in all of which he played the passive or feminine role. His libido is directed primarily at male underwear, which stands as a symbol of the ultra-masculine partner he desires but lacks the courage to seek. He freely admits that he took his present job as an assistant in the haberdashery department of a large department store, in order to be in close contact with male underwear, of which, incidentally, he has an enormous personal collection.

'I always do the underwear displays myself and I'm afraid it excites me terribly. Twice I've been ticked off by the head of the department for padding display briefs too realistically. I can't control my feelings at all. To me a pair of pants is just as exciting as a nude man. More so, in fact. When a good-looking man comes to buy pants from me, I often have an involuntary ejaculation. Just handling them and imagining the customer in them excites me beyond belief. I have a sort of game I play with myself, trying to guess what sort of pants a given man wears. I'm very good at it. I spend hours and go miles out of my way sometimes if I see a man in tight trousers that show the seams of his briefs. I can't take my eyes off them and just follow him in a state of acute excitement. This year, in our annual sale, we had a lot of seconds of briefs in bright colours. All the young lads from the local offices used to come in at lunchtime and inspect them. On several occasions I was able to overhear them discussing the sort of pants they wore. A lot of the men who looked at them would make jokes, saying they were "cissie" and like girls', and then they'd ask each other what sort they wore. Several times during the sale I had an involuntary orgasm.'

There is in Paul R's reactions to his fetish object a great deal of the thrill of experiencing something forbidden. Underwear is, in his mind, still something private and furtively exciting. He enjoys gathering information about other men's under-sartorial habits because he then feels that he possesses some secret knowledge about them. Like Frederick C he is a great observer, an obsessional observer even, of underwear displayed on clothes lines, but he has never stolen any. He also watches very carefully at the local launderette and has a fund of stories about how he has seen various young men putting their soiled underwear

35

into the machines. To him, these observations are deeply sexual, deeply exciting.

Unlike most fetishists, Paul R has a very well-defined theory about the growth of his own addiction which has been borne out by recent information from the U.S.A.

'As a teenager I was terribly conscious of my attraction to my own sex and went out of my way to avoid any possibility of making sexual contacts. I was very nervous, very timid, and I couldn't bear the idea of my friends or anyone finding out what I really thought. I never used to look at the other boys in the changing room at school. I daren't. My only outlet was solitary masturbation, which I used to do while looking at photographs of footballers and athletes in the papers. Then I discovered the physique magazines. When I first discovered the more sexy ones that you only buy around Soho and places like that, I was terribly disappointed that the models weren't nude. I'd thought they would be because I had imagined so often what they must contain before I could pluck up the courage to buy them. Then, when the first real briefs were introduced for men, more and more of the models in these magazines used to be shown wearing them and nearly always with their penes clearly outlined beneath the material. They used to excite me enormously. I began to understand that that was as much as they dare show, and I loved it. I got bolder and used to flip through the magazines before buying them. I'd only buy those that had photographs of boys in underpants for they were the ones that really excited me. I've thought about it a lot and I'm sure that my passion for pants began as a result of those pictures. Up until then I'd never given pants a thought.'

The magazines to which Paul R referred were predominantly American. That country has been the main source of supply of physique magazines, or to give them a more accurate description, homosexual pin-up books, for many years. In the last two years, however, the American publishers have been able to publish full frontal nude pictures of male models in their magazines. These were, at first, extremely successful, but recent trends have indicated that the old revealing studies of models in underwear are again in demand. Nudity of such a flagrantly sexual kind soon palls. It has, obviously, a novelty value, but the concealed genitals, hinted at but not shown, are proving to be more stimulating in the long run. This fact bears out Paul R's theory, and certainly his explanation of his own obsessional interest in male underwear is completely convincing. By exposure to these 'tease-shots' (which are an excellent example of our observations in the last chapter about the erotic power of the semi-clothed figure) his sexual focus has become fixed on underwear and indifferent to the accepted centre of attraction. Obviously, as with all fetishists, this has been encouraged by his timidity and fears of being recognized as a homosexual, and, of course, the pants act as a masculine symbol, just as woman's underwear represents her in the abstract.

So far we have concentrated on the general symbolic aspects of underwear as a substitute for the partner, with only brief references to the intrinsic properties of the garments themselves. Yet these are extremely important. Bart V was deeply affected by the feel of feminine pants and other fetishists are equally concerned with their appearance. For example, one man is only interested in black pants, another only in transparent ones. Some prefer frills and lace, and many older men are indifferent to all but the directoire knickers which were the height of eroticism in their youth. Similarly, a large number of men are only interested in worn and soiled underwear. They are never tempted to steal from washing lines, or to buy pants for themselves. A pair of women's pants are completely uninteresting to them unless they have been worn. This obviously presents a great problem as far as acquisition is concerned. Some men confess to handling their mother's or sister's underwear when it is placed in the wash. Ian S, on the other hand, steals from the local launderette.

'It's quite easy really. A number of women leave their washing for the assistants to deal with and it's usually left lying around for some hours. The assistants are always gossiping or doing something and it's fairly simple to nick a pair of pants when nobody's looking. I've never been caught yet.'

The evidence, visual and particularly odorous, of the garment's having been recently worn obviously brings the female image closer. Ian S, like most of his kind, has no interest in the visual or tactile properties of the pants. It is the knowledge that they have been worn, that they smell of a woman's body, that makes them desirable and exciting. By sniffing the odour retained by the garment, Ian S is able to imagine himself in intimate contact with the wearer.*

'Having got them from the launderette I usually have an idea of the woman who has been wearing them and that, plus the smell, makes it easy for me to imagine being with her and having relations with her. I put the pants on and get very excited by the knowledge that my penis is resting against material that has been stained and perfumed by her vagina.'

This is, in fact, a symbolic form of coitus, or coitus by

* For a detailed analysis of the erotic power of odours, and of odour fetishism, see *The Sweet Smell of Sex* by Richard K. Champion, Canova Press, London, 1969.

proxy via the agency of a used garment. As we would expect, Ian S feels himself inadequate with women and finds it difficult to form even the most casual relationship with them. Instead he has a solitary love affair with the stolen underwear of strangers. He retains these garments for as long as they remain odoriferously redolent, then throws them away and steals another pair. The implanting of this particular fetish in his mind followed the classic pattern.

'I was the only boy in a family of three sisters, and I was very curious about girls when I was around fifteen or so. We had a big laundry basket in our bathroom where we all used to put our dirty clothes for Mum to wash. One day, as I was putting a shirt or something in the basket, I caught sight of a pair of pants belonging to one of my sisters. I don't know why I picked them up, simple curiosity I suppose, but when I did so I got my first whiff of that peculiar, undefinable odour that is the essence of a woman. I was very stimulated and masturbated there and then.

'Thereafter, whenever I had a bath, I used to ransack the laundry basket and smell all the girls' pants I could find and try them on. Nothing else has ever satisfied me like that and never could.'

Ian S's involvement with soiled underwear was, from the very outset, associated with his sisters. The incestuous overtones of this fact were not lost upon him and he tends to equate all women with his sisters. He knows that incest is forbidden and strenuously denies ever having had any desire for his sisters. Yet sex is subconsciously linked with the forbidden sisters and all women are denied him because he compares them to and associates them with his sisters. Thus intercourse with any woman would equate to incest in his eyes, and so he avoids them, relying on smell fetishism via underpants for stimulation and release.

Underwear fetishism can also take the form of a desire to see a woman in her underwear, or in specially selected undergarments. This is, obviously, a form of voyeurism and often takes in the whole range of underclothes and not just one isolated garment. Also, the garments are not especially stimulating by themselves. They must be worn by an attractive woman. Equally, the woman herself is not desired and no attempt is made to have intercourse with her.

Albert P pays periodic visits to a prostitute. With him he takes a black lace, half-cup brassiere, a scarlet suspender belt, a pair of black nylon stockings and a pair of scarlet briefs. The prostitute puts on these garments in a separate room and then 'models' them for him, striking teasing poses and displaying her underwear while he quietly masturbates. Once he is satisfied, the girl returns the garments and Albert P leaves. He makes no other use of the underwear and never wants to have intercourse with the girl, or to have her touch him in any way.

Erotic fiction often exploits this sort of voyeuristic fetishistic interest, as the following quotation demonstrates.

'The swelling of her full, golden breasts was caught by a wisp of coffee-coloured lace, a ridiculous, flimsy scrap of a half-cup bra that let the vermilion tips of her hard-pointed nipples peep through. His eyes travelled down her flat abdomen to the wide, flaring hips where befrilled panties of sensuous white silk masked the hidden treasures of her body. She pirouetted coquettishly on six-inch heels, displaying the firm mounds of her buttocks which pressed tightly against the clinging, almost revealing, silk. Long jet suspenders were taut against her creamy thighs. The contrast of black against white flesh made him gasp for air. They held sheer nylons halfway up her thighs. He saw the tight binding of silk against her swelling mound of Venus.'

40

More distinct fetishism is confined to books which take that deviation as a main theme. In such cases, the detail of the garments is exhaustive, the tone that of an ecstatic lover faced with a new mistress.

'Her precious, precious panties. Like gossamer, as pink as her own perfect buttocks. Like the blush of an early summer rose. Their texture, their supple silkiness exceeded even the softness of her skin. The legs were trimmed with satin bows and ruffles of fine, hand-made lace. His excitement knew no bounds as he raised them tenderly to his face and kissed each flounce and frill, savouring the delicate perfume that clung to them and conjured her into his mind.'

Here the garment clearly stands as a symbol of one beloved woman, which is extremely rare in cases of actual fetishism. Yet the pants are employed fetishistically and treated to kisses which would normally be reserved for their owner.

Erotica is one of the few places where fetishism is associated with women. In reality it is extremely rare to find a woman who shares the masculine love of underwear. But, largely because such books are written by men, for men, women are often endowed with all the traits of fetishism, particularly in novels which have lesbianism as their main concern.

'Her delicious little baby-blue panties! I felt a rush of blood to my head as I grabbed them from her unmade bed. Little gathered nylon pants, trimmed with rows of narrow lace. I held them ecstatically, smelling them, imagining her in my arms. My nipples were hard and a seeping fire dampened the crotch of my own panties. The bed contained the impression of her body. How like a child she must sleep, curled small, snuggled into the softness. I threw myself down on the indentation she had left, pressing my burning body where hers had been. I held the blue, tantalizing panties close to my eyes and explored every inch of them, jealous of their intimacy with her. A golden, curling hair clung to one seam, shed by her secret fleece. I detached it, held it, and then nuzzled my mouth into the fragrant crotch in search of her.'

Here again the garment summons up the image of the desired girl and finally acts as a substitute for her with an act of cunnilingus being performed by proxy. Homosexual erotica is particularly suited to this sort of fetishistic exploitation because invariably the lesbian heroine or homosexual hero cannot profess her or his desire for a member of their own sex and in the ecstasy of their passion a garment, particularly a piece of underwear, brings the frustrated lover into symbolic contact with the unsuspecting object of desire.

'I wished there was some sort of magic that could transform me, for just a few hours, into his jockey-shorts. To spend just a moment cosseting that powerful masculine bulge of his, to rub against the hair-dusted globes of his ass would be ecstasy. To soak up his sweat and the sweet exudations of his body would be bliss. I held his discarded, worn briefs in my hands and envied them. They knew him better, had more intimate knowledge of him than I could ever hope to have.'

The frequency of such fetishistic passages in erotica reveals a tacit understanding on the part of the authors of the sexual symbolism of underwear and of the erotic interest any reference to it can be certain to arouse. It is assumed, and with reason, that all men are interested in underwear as a foretaste of later sexual activity, even though they may not be fetishists.

The fetishist who favours the brassiere is, as one would

42

expect, much less common that the pantie-fetishist. There is an obvious connection with breast fetishism which invariably has its roots in early childhood. The man who becomes excited by viewing and holding a brassiere does so because it conjures up visions of the female breasts. He can fantasize handling them and reaches orgasm as a result of this imaginary manipulation. Invariably such men have some recollection of first connecting their sexual feelings with the display of the breasts. They have, as a result, no interest in the vagina or intercourse, but get real fulfilment the brassiere, and when they do it is employed in much more easily accomplished, and can be done without a woman's awareness of its true effect on the man, such men are generally able to satisfy their need without recourse to fetishism. Only extreme cases fix their sexual focus on the brassière, and when they do it is employed in much the same way as pants are.

Underwear fetishism, like any other form of the aberration, has an obsessive hold on the fetishist which can dominate his whole life. Work, friends, interests, all are sacrificed to the pursuit of the desired object, with orgasm perhaps leading to only a few days' respite before the urge for satisfaction again takes hold of the victim.

'Panties mean nothing to me unless they are worn by a woman. I organize my life to give me as much time as possible to follow my pursuit. I walk the streets waiting to catch a glimpse of a girl's pants under her miniskirt. I could write a book on the best places for viewing women's underwear. I spend hours sitting through films that bore me because the pictures outside have promised a glimpse of a girl in her pants. When, at last, I am sufficiently excited, or, as more often happens, too tired to hunt any

43

more, I go home and review all that I have seen and masturbate over the memories.'

After all this effort, this cruel parody of the male's search for a female, the only reward the victim has is solitary masturbation. Not for him the shared mental and physical companionship of a woman, just a collection of images or impersonal garments which enable him to obtain a brief, fleeting satisfaction. There is seldom little hope of the fetishist marrying, or forming any sort of satisfactory relationship with a woman. Many would not even want to, although their sexual lives are dictated by their failure to do so. But for others, like Bart V, this can be a very acute problem indeed.

'I never considered I had a problem until I got very serious about a girl a year or so back. She was a wonderful person and would have made me a good wife. I know she wanted to marry me, but how could I ask her and then risk having her lose all respect for me when she discovered that I could only do it when I had a pair of lacy pants on? I had to wise up and face the question, what kind of a guy is it who has to wear a pair of girl's pants before he can make love to a woman?'

One with a serious problem, as Bart V came to understand. But few fetishists are able to view their devotion in such a realistic light. They are too intensely aware of their failure with women, or of their fear of women, and they know that it is only their fetish objects that have made possible the small degree of sexual expression they enjoy. Thus their view of any attempt to help them is a prejudiced one. They cannot see beyond the fact that the object of the exercise is to take away the little they have. They dare not trust in their ability to overcome the fear that has driven them to a substitute in the first place, and

44

without the comfort and excitement of that, their lives seem totally bleak. The ever-increasing grip of the fetish, which continually narrows their lives, seems infinitely preferable by contrast.

3: Gloves

CLOTHING and, to a lesser extent, material fetishism is greatly influenced by fashion and trends. For example, twenty or thirty years ago sheet rubber and rubberized fabrics were very easily available, whereas today they have been very largely replaced by plastics with a consequent falling off in the numbers of rubber fetishists. If a material becomes scarce there is, obviously, a considerably reduced danger of the young being exposed to the material in a sexual context. Similarly, the contemporary trends in women's clothing greatly affect the sexual focus, particularly with regard to the already mentioned fact that when the body is virtually covered from neck to ankle, the remaining small areas of exposed flesh become exaggeratedly erotic in contrast. Thus it is not surprising that glove fetishism is comparatively rare today. But in the days of Queen Victoria, and for some time afterwards, when it was believed that no lady should be seen out without her gloves, this apparently asexual garment became a source of delight for a great many men and even for quite a few women. The gloves, it should be remembered, were one of the very few articles of wearing apparel which it was permitted for a lady to take off in company and virtually the only one which then left an area of skin bare. Today we are unlikely even to notice a woman's hands, so accustomed to them are we and so much more of her body is there on display, but if we consider the following Victorian description of a woman, we will be able to understand something of the very different attitude which prevailed only a hundred years ago.

'She was the picture of delicacy, a small woman of refinement and sartorial circumspection. Her gown of watered black silk was decorated at the high collar, cuffs and hem with a pattern of jet beads which caught and reflected the light. The silk was drawn tight over her full bosom, and echoed the tightly-corseted shape of her form even to the first swelling of her hips, from which her skirts depended in voluminous pleats and folds. Her delicate arms were sheathed in the self-patterned silk and closed with six small jet buttons. From the decorated cuffs, her white hands appeared, elegantly shaped and with fine, opalescent nails. How they glowed, as though with some ethereal light, against her black skirt. They lay, quietly folded, in her lap, stark white and naked against the dark, concealing gown then adopted by ladies of quality.'

It will be obvious from this that before we can usefully consider gloves as a fetish object, we must establish the sexual force of the hands which they covered. Gloves were, of course, a symbol of the hands, just as underwear is a symbol of the genitals. The sexual connotations of the latter point is immediately communicable and universally comprehensible, but most of us do not see the hands as a sexual part of the body and we must understand this before we can understand the attraction of gloves.

In our sexually permissive times we tend to take for granted the very important role which the hands inevitably play in any sexual relationship. Lovers use their hands to caress. The accepted start of a sexual relationship is the holding of hands, a symbolic joining which foreshadows the ultimate coupling of intercourse. Lovers arouse each other by caressing their bodies with their hands. Even the brushing of hands can result in an electric shock of desire when two people are strongly attracted. Years ago, to clasp a woman's hand was a sign of very serious affection or desire. It was a habit, in some societies, for a man to kiss a woman's hand and this could be the only form of quasi-sexual contact permitted between the sexes out of wedlock. Therefore, at a time when virtually only the hands were displayed unclothed it is possible to understand how the fundamental sexual usage, i.e. caressing, holding hands, took on a much stronger erotic aspect.

Now, a human being's first experience of a sexual act is invariably auto-masturbation, i.e. the stimulation of the penis or vagina to orgasm by the hand. In this sense, the first sexual organ we discover, other than our own, is our hand. In a society such as that which obtained in Victorian England, all other sexual outlets were effectively blocked, and various serious attempts were made to forbid and frustrate masturbation. However, mankind is not so easily controlled and it cannot be doubted that the war against masturbation, which is always a sign of a truly repressive society, far from stopping these desires, only endowed masturbation with a greater, more furtive, attraction. Today most of us tend to accept masturbation as an essential part of adolescence, out of which we quickly grow. The average human being soon realizes that the hand is a poor sexual substitute for the vagina, and that solitary sex is far less exciting than that which is shared with another person. That is, unless masturbation is forbidden and condemned, which fact, when allied to the prohibition of virtually all other outlets, only makes the act more desirable and more fulfilling.

Let us, for the purposes of demonstration, imagine an ordinary youth living in such a society. His relationships with the opposite sex are seriously limited by what is socially accepted. He is sexually ignorant. But he has discovered that his penis grows erect on occasions and that the pleasurable sensations which he then experiences can be heightened, prolonged and finally brought to a shattering peak of pleasure if he caresses his erection with his hand. Despite all injunctions to shun such 'sinful practices', his penis insists upon becoming erect and will not for long be frustrated. His pleasure increases with the knowledge that he is doing something 'wrong'. He experiences, as a result of this prohibition, a psychological thrill of wickedness and defiance which is curiously linked to his physical arousal. Then he discovers that certain sights cause erections more frequently. He may be watching a young woman, may brush against her skirts or smell her perfume and discover that these sensations excite him sensually. He will recall these sensations when he masturbates and the more he contemplates her, the more his excitement will grow. In his ignorance, he has no idea what the sexual coupling of a man and a woman entails. His mind will not be able to fathom the mysteries of coitus without instruction. He will only know that the pleasurable sensations in his penis are intrinsically connected with the young woman. In his longing he will simply want to be as close to her as possible. He will kiss her, press against her, in his mind that is, but that will not seem enough. At last, with trembling daring, he will imagine her putting her small white hand on his penis, to caress him as he caresses

48

himself. It seems certain to him that the pleasurable sensations he can give himself will be doubled if another's hand, a woman's hand, performs these ministrations for him. This fantasy leads to orgasm and, assuming his attraction towards the woman continues, next time he sees her, her body completely veiled by concealing garments, he will glance guiltily at those, by contrast, shockingly naked hands with a mixture of fear and delight. His mind has already imagined the pleasure they could bring him and it seems inconceivable that she cannot guess his thoughts. His penis grows erect as he contemplates her hands and the memory of them continues to feed his fantasies until, at last, he can stand it no longer. Guiltily, trembling, he snatches her gloves from where they lie in the hall. His motives are probably romantic. The gloves are a keepsake, a reminder of the girl he adores, something he will treasure. But when, in the privacy of his own room, he takes them out to examine them, they evoke in him all the sensual delights his mind has conjured in the past. The gloves that he holds, that have been worn by her, which yet contain some faint trace of her perfume, become linked with his desire. He is already on the way to becoming a glove fetishist.

Glove fetishism, as we can see, is an excellent example of a form of the aberration which is influenced by socio-sexual attitudes and which requires the transference of the sexual focus not simply to a symbol but to a non-sexual part of the body. We may say, therefore, that the glove fetishist not only regards the glove as a substitute for the hand, but the hand itself as a substitute for the vagina. In other words, the hand takes precedence as the main sexual organ, into conjunction with which the penis is brought in a travesty of intercourse.

Of course, as with all fetishes, the intrinsic qualities of

49

the gloves themselves are very important. Dainty lace and cotton gloves are obviously connected with femininity, with the delicate hands of a woman, while tightly fitting leather ones suggest an ambivalent sexuality, being both feminine and masculine at the same time. The actual shape of the gloves excites some people, and odour, as we have already indicated, is often a factor. All these aspects combine for the true glove fetishist who invariably remembers the days when gloves were an essential part of a lady's *toilette* and were as much a mark of romanticized femininity as a lace brassiere is today. The importance of gloves to a woman, and indeed many of the more harmful fads of Victorianism, persisted long after that age had become a subject for the history books, particularly among the upper-middle and upper classes. Today fashions and customs change so quickly that we tend to forget how tenacious the tenets of Victorianism proved themselves to be. There are still many men whose fondness for gloves dates back to what now seems to be a vanished world. One such gentleman commented:

'One noticed a woman's hands in those days. They were a mark of her class. One glance at a woman's hands and one could place her socially. In those days the shops weren't stocked with creams and unguents which nowadays enable a woman to preserve delicate hands even after a day's washing. Women did pamper their hands, of course, those who could. To have nicely shaped hands was a mark of breeding to us, although today I suppose a geneticist would tell us it was nothing of the sort. And one was conscious of them because of the styles women affected.

'I well recall being at a dance when I was quite a young man. I met my future wife there, in fact. She had beautiful arms and I remember being struck by her gloves. In those days women wore sleeveless, low-cut gowns in the evening, but even so a woman of any modesty and fashion covered her arms in long gloves which reached quite to the biceps. This girl was wearing just such a pair, of supple white kid. There was an opening which buttoned from the heel of the palm and proceeded for some inches up the inner arm. At supper time these buttons were undone and the hand slipped free to enable her to eat. Getting those long gloves on and off was quite a business, and it was much more convenient to bare the hand in that fashion.

'I remember how enthralled I was as I watched her pull back the hands in order to eat. It was a garment that drew attention to the hands and inspired the most lascivious thoughts. When I danced with her, I was incensed by the touch of her gloves and beseeched her to give me one as a keepsake. Of course, she refused. There was no other course open to a young woman of standing in those days. But the next morning I purchased an even finer pair and sent them to her with a declaration of my feelings. In return, I begged the ones she had worn that night. She sent them and they were my most treasured possession for many years.'

Such reminiscences do seem to invoke a lost world which, for all its superficial and charming romanticism, was a seething morass of frustrated desires which provided a perfect place for the development of fetishism of all kinds. The point made about long evening gloves is particularly interesting. These gloves were often made of lace or some other diaphanous material. Often the arm, although officially exposed, was completely covered save for a strip of flesh between the top of the glove and the bottom of the sleeve. This is, in fact, another good example of the teasing nature of clothes, of woman's apparently instinctive habit

51

of hinting at much but revealing little. The arm so clothed, of course, takes on a similarity to the stockinged leg, with the aforementioned band of flesh being as erotic as the much praised gap between stocking top and the underwear. If we consider this comparison, we can possibly understand a little of the erotic excitement generated by such revelations when the rest of the body was concealed.

Today one of the most revealing sources of information about glove fetishism is erotica. It may surprise the modern reader to know that many works were written years ago which took glove fetishism as their main theme. One such, *The Gloved Goddess*, demonstrates the point about the long evening glove.

'She stood close to him, but a little in front and half-turned towards the lighted room beyond. Her arm, so plump and firm, almost touched his chest. Her hands were linked loosely together, resting against the stiff brocaded skirt of her gown. She wore gloves like cobwebs, with golden thread caught in the pattern of the lace. They reached almost to the edges of the puffed sleeves of her dress, but before they did so, they left bare an inch-wide strip of her flesh, the very consummation of that which glowed radiantly through the holes in the pattern of her gloves.

'Feverishly trembling, he laid his finger on this exposed patch of flesh. He felt her quiver in response. She glanced, startled, at him, and then returned her gaze to the room. She unclasped her hands and let them drop to her sides. It was now his turn to be startled, for her wrist brushed the front of his trousers and sent chills of fire racing through his veins. She began to unbutton the wrist of her right glove. He, meanwhile, could resist no longer. Stooping, he laid his trembling lips to that precious gap between sleeve and glove. His attention was caught, however, by her raised hand. Meaningfully, she held her hand before his eyes and rolled back the dainty hand of the glove into a tight roll around her wrist. She wriggled her fingers under his nose.

' "I see," she said coquettishly, "that my reputation has reached your ears. Well, look then, here is the gentlemen's comforter," and before his astonished eyes she dropped her hand and began to unbutton his trousers.'

The Gloved Goddess, as may be supposed from that extract, concerns a woman, married to a much older man, who makes a habit of masturbating the various men in her social circle. She will permit no other intimacy, but enslaves them with the skill and power of her hand. The bulk of the book, however, is taken up with loving descriptions of her gloves.

'He caught the twinkle in her dark eyes as, never ceasing in the exchange of pleasantries with his aunt, she began to draw off her gleaming black kid gloves, glancing from time to time in his direction in order to satisfy herself that the full impact of her tantalizing was not lost upon him.

'Seizing the tips of each finger in her other hand, she loosed the fingers in turn, working methodically from thumb to little finger until, with a gesture at once defiant and revelatory, she had loosened it sufficiently to draw the glove quite off. Then she recommenced the procedure with the other hand.

'A groan escaped him. He wriggled in his chair.

' "Why, Mr. Sampson," she said, looking full at him, "whatever ails you? Are you unwell? Pray, what is it?" '

As with all fetishistic fiction, the fetish is treated as the beloved. The act of handling or removing the gloves is described with the detail and rapture which is reserved for the description of sexual acts in more straightforward examples of the *genre*. It is erotic fiction, too, which gives us a glimpse of what the fetishist does with the gloves once he has got them.

'With trembling hands, Algernon tore at the buttons of his clothes, dropping them where he stood until his aching manhood waggled free before him. Then and only then did he take out the glove Lucy had dropped in the park that afternoon and which had obsessed his thoughts from the moment he had retrieved it. Now he held it in his palm, so small in comparison to his own rough hand, and wrapped it around his masculine stem. A thrill of delight emanated from his groin and diffused his whole body. Seizing himself, he moved the glove slowly, teasingly, up and down his engorged flesh until a violent shaking seized his whole frame and his head swam with lascivious thoughts.'

The casebooks of the earliest sexological researchers contain frequent references to instances of glove fetishism whereas in a comparable contemporary work such cases are conspicuous by their absence. This, of course, demonstrates the fact that glove fetishism is, in these days of almost total bodily exposure, very rare indeed. As a result, these early accounts must furnish us with details of the aberration.

'Patient was a sturdy man, aged forty-six, with normal physical development. He suffered from severe headaches and temporary loss of memory. Was extremely affected by the sight of women's gloves, which he frequently stole from their owners. The headaches and loss of memory followed these criminal acts.

'At the age of five or six, the patient recalled pleasurable emotions when his mother came to bid him good night before leaving for some evening engagement. The patient would seize her gloved hand and hold it as long as possible, often covering it with kisses in order to detain

54

his beloved mamma. These incidents were early accompanied by pleasurable sensations in the genitals and perineum. He would feign tears and restlessness in order to keep his mother by his side and encourage her to soothe his forehead and throat with her gloved hand.

'At fourteen, the patient began to masturbate, accompanying the act with recollections of his mother's gloves. He began to steal gloves from his mother's room and would wear these when practising self-pollution. When the patient was sent away to school, these practices ceased and for some time he experienced no desire for contact with gloves.

'After military service, the patient fell in love with a young woman whom he admired for her fine hands and delicate gloves. He experienced involuntary ejaculation when fondling, holding and kissing her gloved hand. Patient married the young woman in his twenty-ninth year. He attempted to persuade his wife to perform masturbation on him while wearing gloves. The wife refused and subsequently denied him all marital rights.

'He began to frequent prostitutes whom he paid to masturbate him while wearing gloves. He frequently became excited when out walking with his wife and contemplating her gloved hands. He frequently made presents of gloves to his wife and stole them back after she had worn them. In recent years he has been unable to resist the impulse to steal gloves from female relations and acquaintances. All these he employs for purposes of self-manipulation.

'At the time of consultation, the patient had become feverish and restless when in the company of a woman with gloved hands. He stole more and more frequently and after employing these articles for sensual gratification

55

would experience painful headaches and temporary loss of memory.'

This classic case shows how the patient learned as a child to connect gloves with sex. This deviation was obviously greatly aggravated by his wife's reaction against his fetishism and, by being denied, the desire achieved unmanageable proportions. It is obvious from this clearly reported case that glove fetishism is born and nurtured by similar circumstances to that of underwear or any other fetishism. The social niceties of the time dictated late marriages without offering the average male any alternative sexual outlet. This obviously allowed the fetish to develop its hold and the patient completely failed to transfer his sexual focus from his wife's gloves to the proper centre of attraction. By refusing to indulge his sexual tastes, she only drove him into greater dependency upon his fetish object. The headaches and temporary loss of memory are obviously an attempt to escape and punish himself for his addiction. Both were physical symptoms caused by his fetishism and the guilt he felt as a result.

Another case history, reported many years ago, concerned a youth of sixteen who was described as having 'an unusually long and extremely thin penis. As a result of this physical development, the patient was able to draw the middle finger of a lady's glove over his erect *membrum*, which procedure afforded him great stimulation and pleasure. He would wear a glove in this fashion under his usual clothing and could, as a result of stimulating contact with the glove, maintain his aroused state for upwards of two hours. When sufficiently excited, the youth would retire to a private place, expose himself and rapidly move the tight finger of the glove up and down on his organ until he had an emission into the glove itself.'

This boy had been apprehended for molesting women in the street. He had caught hold of their gloved hands and pressed them to his groin. As a result he had been recommended for psychiatric treatment. The boy was ill-educated and had amassed an astonishingly large collection of stolen gloves. By polluting the gloves in the way described, the boy was obviously revenging himself upon the female. His lack of education was said to make him feel that women rejected him. He was also, we are told, an ugly boy whose advances had been rejected by young girls of his own class. The source of his glove fetishism was traced to the following incident.

'One night, some two years before his case came to our attention, the youth had been roaming around the town with an unsupervised group of his peers. Near the river they had witnessed a gentleman soliciting one of the prostitutes who haunt the bridges in that area of the town. The man, having made his bargain, had leaned against a wall and exposed his organ. The prostitute, at his bidding, had taken it in her gloved hand, masturbating him to orgasm, which act the boys witnessed to completion.'

The boy, whom we may conclude was somewhat simple, obviously thought that this act was what normally took place between a man and a woman, a fact which explains why, in his unsuccessful attempts to seduce young girls, he had exposed his erect penis and tried to persuade them to hold it. It is not surprising, given this background, that his frustration should lead him to a complex form of glove fetishism.

Krafft-Ebing in his pioneering *Psychopathia Sexualis* recounts a case which has many similarities to those which we have already cited.

'X, thirty-three years old, a manufacturer from America,

57

who has been living for eight years in a happy marriage, blessed with children, consulted me regarding a most remarkable glove fetishism which was tormenting him, on account whereof he was forced to despise himself and which might well drive him to despair and madness. X appears to have come from a perfectly healthy family, but since his infancy has been a neuropathic and easily excitable man. He describes himself as of a very sensual nature, while his wife is, he says, *natura frigida*.

'At the age of about nine, misled by his companions, he began masturbating. He found great pleasure in this and gave himself up passionately to it. One day, while he was vigorously excited he found a little sack made out of chamois leather. He drew this over his *membrum* and experienced thereby an extreme, pleasant sensation. He used it now for onanistic manipulation, laid it on his scrotum, too, and wore it on him day and night. From then on there awoke in him a great interest in leather generally and quite especially for glacé gloves. From puberty onwards it was only leather *women's gloves* which made a quite fascinating impression on him, produced erection, and if he was so situated that he could touch his penis with them, to ejaculation too. Men's gloves had not the slightest charm for him, though he gladly carried them on his own body.

'It came to be only the gloves that interested him in women. It became his fetish, and glacés in particular, as long as possible, with plenty of buttons, but particularly when they were dirty, greasy with fat, marked with sweat marks on the finger-tips. Women got up in this manner, even if ugly and old, did not escape exerting a certain charm on him. Ladies with gloves of material or silk left him quite cold. Ever since puberty he had been accustomed to stare at women, primarily their hands. Otherwise he was little interested in them. If he chanced to press the hand of a lady with glacé gloves, he had a sensation of "warm, gentle" leather, and with it, erection and orgasm. If he was able to gain possession of a lady's glove of that kind, he would proceed with it to the closet, wrap his genitalia in it, then draw it off again and masturbate. Later, in the brothel, he used to take long gloves with him, begged the prostitutes to put these on, and was so excited by this that quite often the ejaculation followed at once.

'X became a collector of ladies' glacé gloves. He had hidden away, in one place or another, hundreds of pairs of them. In hours of leisure he used to count them and contemplate them with admiration, as a miser does his pieces of eight, he put them over his genitals, hid his face in heaps of gloves, then pulled one on to his hand and masturbated, experiencing more pleasure in the process than in coitus. He made himself penis-coverings, suspensories, preferably out of soft, black leather, and wore them all day. Furthermore, he fixed women's gloves on a sling so that they covered his genitalia like an apron.

'After his marriage, his glove fetishism got sharper and sharper. Normally he was only potent if during the marital act he had a pair of his wife's gloves lying near his head, so that he could kiss them. His wife made him quite delighted if she allowed herself to be persuaded to draw on gloves for coitus and as a preliminary to touch his genitals with them. At the same time, X was feeling quite unhappy about his fetishism and made frequent but ever vain efforts to liberate himself from the "charm of gloves".

'If ever he met the word "glove", or a picture of one, in a novel, fashion paper, or newspaper it used to exert at times a simply fascinating effect on him. At the theatre, his gaze was riveted on the actress' hands. He could scarcely be torn away from the display windows of glove shops. He often felt driven to stuff big gloves with wool, etc., so as to make them resemble clothed arms. It is among his habits to carry female glacé kid gloves around with him, and to wrap up his genitalia at night with them, until he feels his penis like a great leather Priapus in between his legs.

'When in big towns he buys from glove laundries ladies' gloves which have not been collected, i.e. are owner-less – preferably thoroughly dirty and worn out. On two occasions the otherwise correct Herr X confesses he was unable to resist the desire of stealing them. When in crowds he cannot resist the urge to stroke ladies' hands; at his office he uses every opportunity of shaking hands with ladies so as to be able to feel for a second the "warm and blessed" leather. He begs his wife to wear glacé or leather gloves whenever she can. And he provides her abundantly with gloves of those kinds. In his office X always has ladies' gloves lying about. Never an hour passes without his hav-ing to stroke or touch them. When particularly excited sensually, he sticks a glove of the sort into his mouth and chews on it. Other objects of female *toilette*, as also parts of the female body other than the hands, have not the slightest attraction for him.'

This long account demonstrates just about every aspect of glove fetishism and may justly be regarded as a classic of its kind. It shows how haphazard the discovery of the object can be, how exclusive the preference within the general category of objects, and how strange and diverse are the uses to which the fetish can be put. In this as in other cases we have discussed, there appears to be no fear or rejection of women. The fetish cannot really be considered as a substitute for the woman but rather is it completely associated with sexual activity, acting more as a charm to ensure potency and virility.

However, glove fetishism is not completely unknown in our own time. Isolated cases come to the attention of researchers and it is interesting to note that here, as historically, glove fetishism is again closely reflective of socio-sexual attitudes. One of the most remarkable cases concerns a young American, Richard K, who gave this account of his exposure to gloves as a sexual object.

'I was brought up in a small mid-west town and went to high school there. The climax of the high school year in America is the senior prom, a sort of dance and graduation ceremony combined. It is an important social occasion but also a time when the kids kick over the traces. It's very important who you take to the prom, and in my case there was a big conflict. I wanted to take one girl, my parents insisted that I escort another, who happened to be the daughter of their best friends. The thing was that after the prom was regarded as a time for sex, as far as we guys were concerned, so I wanted to take a girl I knew would play along. Valerie, my parents' choice, had a reputation of being a dead loss in the sex stakes. Oh, she was pretty enough and nice enough, but any guy who'd ever dated her got no more than a few chaste kisses. Since her reputation was so well known, I knew all the guys would be laughing at me. Still, I had to take her and both our parents were delighted. We made a beautiful couple, as far as they were concerned.

'It was a drag, but I put a good face on it despite the pitying, ribald remarks of my friends. After the prom, I drove Valerie out of town to one of the recognized necking spots. She went along O.K. because it was part of the ritual of senior prom. From the reputation point of view, it was worse not to go than to go.

'Now you should understand that senior proms were very formal affairs. The girls wore long dresses and gloves. Valerie had on a white dress and little wrist-length white nylon gloves. Very dainty, feminine little things.

'Well, we got to the parking place and I began kissing her. She went along for a little while and I began to think maybe it wasn't so bad after all. She even let me feel her breasts after a while, and I began to get really heated up. But when I put my hand under her skirt, boy, she acted like an iceberg. She pushed my hand away, sat up and called an end to all necking. By this time I was really worked up and I laid it on her good and strong. I told her she was a tease, that I hadn't wanted to bring her anyway and I was damned if I was going to be the only guy in school that night who didn't get his rocks off.

'She was pretty upset by that and I jerked my erection out of my pants and asked her what the hell she was going to do about it. She gave me all the usual crap about saving herself until she met the right guy, etc., so I told her to get down and use her mouth. I knew that a lot of the girls who wanted to hang on to their virginity did that, but oh no, Miss Valerie couldn't do a thing like that. By this time I was desperate and practically begged her to take care of me somehow. So she did. She reached over and put her little gloved hand around the base of my erection. She didn't know how to do it but the feel of that slippery nylon glove on my distended flesh drove me wild. It was the biggest thrill I'd ever had. So I made her make a fist of her hand around my penis and just slide her hand up and down, not moving the foreskin but just brushing my erection with that nylon glove. I held her other hand in mine, feeling the glove with my hand as well as down there. It drove me out of my mind and at last I had a shattering climax. I was so excited, so grateful that I thanked Valerie and apologized for all the mean things I'd said. She'd completely conquered me with her gloves.'

Two things stand out from this account, the formality of the dress that was *de rigueur* on these occasions and the curious dual standards of American courting behaviour. Reputation is extremely important and these two irreconcilable needs – the girl's insistence on retaining her virginity and the boy's equally strong insistence that unless a girl will give him some form of sexual release she is undesirable – often lead to bizarre and even perverted practices. The socio-sexual attitude demands that a girl be both pure and a good sport and that a boy must prove himself as a sexual animal. This dichotomy is closely linked to the concept of reputation and the whole pattern has a public air. In this particular instance, it led Richard K on the path to glove fetishism.

'I went on dating Valerie partly, I told myself, to please my parents and hers and partly to prove to my friends that I had succeeded with her where they had failed, but really it was because I longed to repeat that night's experience with her. She always wore gloves, kid, cloth, cotton, lace and nylon. I loved them all. After that night she had no hesitation in taking care of me, but I always insisted that she keep her gloves on and I became more and more enslaved. I was perfectly happy with Valerie's performance. I got all the sex I wanted and it was sex that completely satisfied me.

'That fall I went away to college and what should have provided me with a whole new series of sexual experiences was a complete disaster. Several girls let me do

63

what I wanted and I was O.K. up until the moment of truth, and then I wanted a gloved hand on my penis. If I couldn't have that I just lost interest. So now *I* began to get a reputation. One night, I asked a girl if she'd do it for me with her gloves on. She just looked at me and said, "What's with you? You some kind of kook or something?" I never asked again. I didn't even try any more. Instead I began buying gloves, girl's gloves, and using them to masturbate myself.

'In the Christmas vacation I picked up with Valerie again and I can't tell you the relief when she took care of me again, wearing a pair of long lace gloves. From that time on I lived for opportunities to be with Valerie. I began to worship her gloves and made her presents of them. It was sort of taken for granted that we should marry and once we were engaged Valerie the iceberg thawed. But I didn't want it any other way and this time it was me who pleaded that we should wait. Valerie thought she had reformed me and agreed. And so we went on the same old way, only now it was so bad I only had to look at her gloved hands to get an erection.

'Well, the wedding-night was a disaster. Valerie turned out to be a very demanding woman. I slowly realized that all those years of taking care of me had been very frustrating for her. But all I wanted was for her to put on a pair of gloves and take care of me like she always had. It's no basis for marriage, though, but what can I do about it? Eventually we reached a sort of compromise. I discovered that if Valerie put on gloves when she was nude and excited me, then guided me into her with her gloved hand, I could manage. But not very often and I couldn't hold out for very long. All this only increased her frustration, of course, and she soon began to take lovers. I can't do anything about it. I can't satisfy her, and she has a right to a proper sex life. But it's a hell of a situation. She spends more and more time with her guys and I'm reduced to masturbating with a pair of her gloves, just like I was back at college.'

This is indeed a sad story and shows how easy it is to pursue the satisfying fetish, which originally began as a compromise to a difficult social problem, instead of insisting upon some less dangerous form of satisfaction. This compromise, dictated by opposed socio-sexual attitudes, has caused both Richard K and his wife a great deal of misery, frustration and sadness. Their marriage is a sham and they are completely unable to break the pattern which was established so unfortunately in their courting days.

Another contemporary case concerns a homosexual youth. The boy's sexual impulse was directed towards his own sex from the very beginning. His earliest masturbation fantasies concerned speculation about older men. His first actual experience with a man occurred when he was fifteen. He had been deliberately seeking some sexual contact and was masturbated by a middle-aged man wearing soft leather gloves. The boy accepted the gloves as a normal part of the act. He believed, since he had been told that masturbation was bad, that the penis was dirty and that the man had kept his gloves on in order to avoid touching him with his hand. Besides, he found the sensation of leather on his penis very exciting. His fetishism, however, is just as limiting as it is to heterosexual men. He has had very few contacts because most people do not want to wear gloves. He actively dislikes being touched by a bare hand and refuses to touch anyone else's penis unless he is allowed to wear gloves. Oral acts fill him with disgust. As a result, he is, to the majority, an unsuccessful partner, and his main outlet is now solitary masturbation, with the aid of gloves.

Of course, the importance of the hands is more easily comprehensible in homosexual relationships. It is not a substitute for the vagina, but the obvious instrument of masturbation between two men. It is the most common homosexual activity and it is easy to see how a homosexual can become fixed upon the hand or glove. However, it is extremely rare, since the majority of homosexuals prefer more sophisticated acts, as is demonstrated by this youth's lack of success in finding partners willing to indulge his glove fetishism.

In 1897, a rare case of glove fetishism concerning a woman was recorded in Austria. The report reads as follows:

'Mrs X had been very much in love with her husband who was killed in a mountaineering accident, leaving her a widow at the comparatively young age of thirty-nine. Her love for her husband was so deep that she had never considered re-marrying, being left a comfortable income and having only two daughters to raise. She preserved her husband's memory intact. Her home contained all his clothes and possessions which she cherished and kept in good repair.

'She had a particular predilection for her husband's gloves, of which she had preserved several pairs. A fastidious man, he had been, during his life, most particular about his gloves. Mrs X was in the habit of fondling these, of smelling them and claimed that this contact brought her husband closer to her. The smell and feel of her husband's gloves excited her, but she was completely indifferent to those belonging to other men, women or new gloves. In moments of great excitement, she would roll her husband's gloves into a ball and press them against her Mons Veneris, closing her thighs about them in order to maintain a steady pressure.'

In this case the gloves are a very definite symbol of one person. Gloves as a whole did not appeal to the woman. She used them simply to invoke her husband's memory. This is typical of the female psyche which tends always to fix on one person and for whom sexual symbols are relatively unimportant save in their ability to bring the loved one closer. Being left a widow so young must have led to a considerable amount of sexual frustration which would explain the use of the gloves in these semi-masturbatory acts. By so employing them the woman would undoubtedly be able to imagine that she was making love with her husband. All other men being apparently repugnant to her, it is inevitable that she should employ some form of symbolism to invoke her husband. If she may be regarded as a glove fetishist at all, hers must certainly be considered a mild case.

The same sort of involvement is apparent in a second case reported many years ago, although the consequences were much more disturbing and the glove fetishism is only a part of a more serious imbalance.

'A serving maid of sixteen, a virgin, somewhat squat of figure and plain of face, conceived a passionate love for the eldest son of her master. She offered herself to the young man on several occasions and in an unequivocal manner. He rejected her, but since he bore the girl no malice, he did not complain of her behaviour. She confided to the cook of the household that he and he alone would have her maidenhead. The cook attempted to reason with her and encouraged her to seek a partner among her own class.

'The girl continued to plague the young man who, in

consequence, tried his best to avoid her. The girl stole a pair of gloves from his room as a keepsake and told her fellow servants that he had made her a present of them. She held the gloves frequently, sniffed them and carried them in the bosom of her dress, maintaining always that the man loved her and would make her his mistress when he came into his fortune. Needless to say, the youth had no such intentions and was annoyed at the loss of the gloves, although he did not suspect the girl of having taken them.

'One day the girl cut the middle finger from the gloves and whittled a piece of wood to fit it. She covered the wood with the leather finger and used this instrument to break her hymen, occasioning herself considerable pain and loss of blood in the process. She announced to her fellow servants, in a delirious state, that the young master had at last taken her maidenhead.'

This poor girl was committed to an asylum as a result of this escapade. Again she cannot be regarded as a true glove fetishist. She had no interest in gloves other than as a symbol of her beloved. This apparently reasonless passion may be regarded as a symptom of her general imbalance, and the act of self-defloration, with the aid of the finger cut from the gloves, as the climax of her fantasy relationship with the young man. In such circumstances, it is obvious that the girl would seek to employ some symbol of the man she loved and the glove finger, in its resemblance to the phallus, is an ideal choice.

Today there can be no doubt that glove fetishism is a rapidly waning aberration. Not only are gloves no longer a required part of a woman's *toilette* but they have become much more functional and, besides, the sexual focus is by no means attracted towards them since so much more

of the body is freely displayed. There are, of course, isolated cases and probably always will be as long as gloves
exist, but they can no longer be regarded as a major source
of fetishistic attraction. These things, however, go in waves
and it is not at all beyond the bounds of possibility that
fashion will, at some time in the future, refocus attention
on the hands and gloves. If this happens, then undoubtedly
some men will have a sexual response to them. Indeed, it
is interesting to note that the recent introduction of leather
gloves which leave part of the back of the hand and even
the knuckles visible, has been cited as sexually exciting
by a number of men. These gloves exploit the principal of
striking a balance between concealment and display, and
since such exposure cannot be functional in an English
winter, we can assume that this is yet another example of
female adornment. At a time when women's clothes are
becoming longer and longer, e.g. the maxi and midi styles,
it is not at all impossible that gloves, in their new, fashion-
able cut-away form, will become again an object of erotic
interest.

4: Boots and Shoes

LIKE gloves, fetishism centred on boots and shoes is greatly
influenced by current fashions. But there are considerable
and important differences between the two kinds of fetishism. Obviously enough shoes were an object of adornment
when women wore long skirts, for the sight of a neat foot
attractively shod was undoubtedly appealing when it

peeped out from beneath a crinoline or some other ankle-length fashion. Women, then, drew attention to their feet and man, as usual, proved to be susceptible. But unlike gloves boots and shoes have never gone out of fashion or ceased to be fetish objects. This is obviously primarily because one can do without gloves but not without shoes. They have, in that sense, always been with us, no matter what the length of skirts, and designers have always found some new innovation with which to capture the attention.

When skirts were shortened, the shape of a woman's legs became extremely important. It was quickly discovered that high heels improved the shape of bad legs and enhanced the natural contours of good ones. That desirable swelling of the calf, that neatness of ankle and tenseness of thigh which is so much admired is, unfortunately, not naturally given to all women, but high heels could do much to alter the stress of the leg muscles to an acceptable approximation of the desired shape. Consequently, heels became higher and higher, and ever more precarious, a danger, some declared, to limb and property. Thus shoes, even with the exposure of those inches of leg which had been covered for centuries, still remained an important feature of a woman's attractiveness, finishing the leg off neatly and improving the shape.

More recently, skirts have been raised and heels lowered. The practicalities of modern living made the stiletto heel undesirable for most women while medical opinion was quick to condemn them as a potential danger. Shoes have suffered something of an eclipse as more and more of the thighs was revealed. Instead women were encouraged to hide the defects of their legs, or draw attention to their shapeliness by wearing calf, knee and thigh length boots. These boots were not only immediately attractive but also

70

practical, providing warmth and protection for the legs that were so dramatically exposed by the advent of the miniskirt. They, of course, focused the attention even more on the female feet and legs, to such an extent that the erotic appeal of boots was celebrated in a successful book.*

As we have frequently said, a fetish is primarily effective in proportion to its ability to evoke that part of the body which it covers. Thus, obviously, boots and shoes are intimately connected with the erotic appeal of the feet and legs. And as we saw with hands, it is perfectly possible for a non-sexual part of the body to be regarded as the object of sexual focus. There are indeed some who are excited by the female foot, although obviously not for any active sexual potential it has. The foot cannot, except in very bizarre instances, be regarded as an object of sexual manipulation. Its charm, for those who admire it, lies rather in its shape and intrinsic odour. It is one of those mysteries why men should react so strongly to the shape of the female foot, but the fact remains that many do. It has been suggested, although without receiving much credence, that the shape of the foot and the shoe subliminally echoes that of the vagina. Doubtful as this claim is, it should not be completely ignored, for a fetishist can seize upon any, and the most unlikely, qualities of his favoured object as a source of attraction. However, it is much more likely that it is the general smallness and delicacy of the female foot in comparison with the heavy, ugly masculine one which is the main source of attraction. This point was, of course, exaggerated when skirts were long and several feet in diameter at the hem. They made the female foot seem even smaller, more delicate. These facts symbolize the basic

* See *Pussies in Boots* by Kidge Wurdak and Kurt Muller, Luxor Press, London, 1968.

concept of femininity, a certain frail vulnerability which appeals sexually to men.

Furthermore, as most of us know to our cost, the feet sweat profusely and, largely because they are protected from the air by stockings and tight-fitting shoes, they smell. To most of us this odour is unpleasant and undesirable. But to some it is a highly erotic perfume, one which is instantly connected in the mind with sexual images and feelings. Thus the odour appears pleasant and even exciting. This is frequently and sometimes the sole factor in the fetishist's attraction.

The legs, of course, which are brought into focus by long boots, have a much more easily recognizable erotic aura. Legs, by virtue of their concealment for so long, have always been an admired and acknowledged erotic part of the female body. They have been described, wittily if not poetically, as the pathway to the vagina, a phrase which reflects the time-honoured, fashion-dictated habit of the male putting his hand beneath a woman's skirts and on to her legs in his quest for access to the genitalia. And, of course, legs, unlike feet, are commonly accepted as attractive limbs in themselves. All these factors are enhanced and given a degree of erotic exaggeration when the legs are clothed in clinging, shining boots.

But any consideration of boots and shoes as fetish objects necessitates the examination of another, less easily defined aspect of fetishism which is, in all probability, more important than any of these physical attributes. We are referring to what might best be described as the psychological 'message' of the fetish object, i.e. the thoughts, images and feelings which, through association and common usage, the objects apparently automatically invoke in the observer. So important are these 'messages', these induced feel-

ings, that we might usefully approach boot and shoe fetishism from two separate angles, that already discussed which
is predominantly concerned with the physical attributes
of the fetish-object, and that which is primarily motivated
by the feelings and emotions released by the visual and
tactile contemplation of the fetish object.

Man has ever confused the idea of worship with self-
abasement. Because he early learned to fear his gods, simply
because their godliness sprang from their greater power
and incomprehensibility, he sought to propitiate them by
stressing his own worthlessness. In order to adore, man
knelt, or prostrated himself, he grovelled and crawled. The
most widely accepted sign of his adoration and of his
consequent self-abasement was, from earliest times, the
kissing of the idol's feet. In this way man admitted his un-
worthiness and showed ultimate respect.

Now we frequently say of man that he 'adores' this or
that woman, that he 'worships the ground on which she
walks', and in most cases we are guilty of a permissible
linguistic exaggeration which conveys the depth of the
man's love. But it is also true that there are men who literally adore and worship women and their sexual impulse
is strangely linked to the idea of self-debasement. We call
such people masochists, by which we mean that their
sexual pleasure is perceived through mental and/or physical pain. Consequently, if a man does truly find pleasure
in the act of worshipping a woman, it is instinctive for him
to kneel, to prostrate himself at her feet and to kiss them.
He thus declares his humility and places himself in her
power.

From this it is obvious that boots and shoes have become linked with this idea of masochistic self-denigration.
The masochist who worships his mistress invites her to

tread upon him to exert her power and, thus, shoe and boot fetishism are very often and very strongly linked with these ideas. Boots have further connotations of dominance and power, of, in fact, sadism which is, of course, the natural complement of masochism. The Nazi jackboot, the military boot, the riding boot, all have connotations of cruelty and power. Thus boots often give the susceptible fetishist the 'message' of domination, inspire in him feelings of fear and reverence for a symbolic power which is so much greater than his own. Consequently, we frequently discover that instances of shoe and boot fetishism are closely linked with masochistic impulses. The classic fetishist will, of course, desire pleasure from both the physical and the psychological aspects of boots and shoes, but there are also many cases where shape and odour, for example, are unimportant and *vice versa*. Yet, as Krafft-Ebing says in his *Psychopathia Sexualis*, 'Shoe fetishism is almost unthinkable without masochistic components,' and goes on to quote the detailed statement of a man whose masochistic involvement with shoes has justly been regarded as a classic example.

'If I meet a woman who seems to me attractive, my wish is not to have sexual intercourse with her in the ordinary sense but to lie on my back on the floor and be trodden on by her feet. This remarkable wish seldom comes off, only when the object of my wonder is a real lady and of beautiful build. She must be elegantly dressed, preferably in an evening cloak, must have pretty high heels and low shoes, either open so that the instep is visible or else fastened by a single strap or band. The edges of the skirt must be raised high enough to give me the view of the foot and observe a fair amount of ankle area, but certainly not as high up as the knee or above it, for then the effect will be

74

diminished. Thus if in fact I often do admire a witty or beautiful woman, no other parts of her really exercise any sexual effect on me than her leg from the knee downwards and the foot; furthermore she must be very carefully dressed. In these conditions there arises in me the wish for sexual gratification by contact with that part of a woman which interests me. Comparatively few women have a leg or a foot beautiful enough to keep me seriously persistent; when however this is the case, or when I imagine it, then I spare no expense or time or other effort to get under her feet, and wait with anxious tension to be trodden on with the greatest energy.

'The trampling must last some minutes and must cover the breast, the abdomen, the inguinal area, and finally the penis too, which when in a state of strong erection along the abdomen is of too firm a consistency to suffer harm from the compression. I also have, for the rest, great pleasure if my throat is compressed by a woman's foot.

'If finally the lady keeps her face towards me and presses with the house shoe of one foot on my penis, so that the high heel rests more or less on the scrotal end of the penis, while the sole covers the major part of the rest, with the other foot on the abdomen, so that I can see and feel the foot sinking in, and then she shifts her weight from that one foot to the other, ejaculation ensues almost immediately. This is in the circumstances described a storm of delight for me, in the course of which the lady's whole weight must be borne straight on to the penis.

'A reason for my peculiar enjoyment of this kind of contact seems to be that first the heel and then the sole of the shoe which is trampling on me impedes the sperm's flowing through and thus considerably draws out the pleasurable excitation. A remarkable mental phenomenon is also to be observed on such occasions. I gladly imagine to myself that the lady who is trampling upon me is my mistress-commandant and I her slave, and that she is doing it in order to punish me for a fault I have committed or in order to contrive pleasure for herself, not me.

'It follows thence that the greater the severity with which I am "punished", the greater my pleasure will be. The concept of "punishment" or of "slavery" seldom arises if I have great difficulty in realizing my wish, but if the person trampling on me is unusually beautiful and heavy the trampling is pitiless.

'I have often been trampled upon so long and so unmercifully that sometimes, when the shoe was placed upon my aching body, I tried to get away from it and was black and blue all day. I have made the greatest efforts to persuade women to act in this manner whenever I believe that I am not thereby insulting them, and I've had astonishingly good luck with it. I must have lain under the feet of at least a hundred women, many of whom came from really good society and would never have even thought of allowing ordinary sexual intercourse, but who were so stimulated or diverted by the idea of carrying it out in this way, that they did it often and repeatedly. I scarcely need say that on the orgasm being induced in this manner, neither my clothes nor those of the ladies were displaced and disordered. After long and multifarious experience, I can solemnly say that my favourite weight is about sixty-five kilograms, and that black shoes with very high heels and brown silk stockings seem to give me the greatest pleasure and awake the strongest desires in me.

'Boots or walking shoes do not distract me nearly to the same degree, albeit on a few occasions I have felt considerable pleasure through their employment. Naked women repel me; I find no pleasure in seeing women in trousers. I do not despise normal sexual intercourse and occasionally practise it. But it means far less pleasure for me than being trodden on. I have also great pleasure – and generally strong erection – when I see a woman who, as I have already described above, must be fully dressed and who is standing on something under her feet – for instance on the foot-pad in a carriage or on the foot-rest of an armchair, etc. I have often hurried along behind a couple of pretty ladies at a picnic or a garden party, simply and solely to see if the grass they've trodden on is slowly standing up again after their feet have stamped it down. And I also see with pleasure the step of a coach beneath a lady – as being something which demands pressure with the feet. I will now explain how it was that my feeling turned in this direction.

'When I was a boy of about fourteen, I once found myself on a long visit to one of my parents' friends. The daughter of the house – the only child – a strong and pretty girl, about six years older than I – was my main playmate. The girl was always prettily dressed, had elegant feet and ankles and, of course, knew it. When it was possible she dressed in such a manner that her best features showed up well – that is to say with ankle shoes with high heels – and was inclined to display these things in a very entertaining and coquettish manner. She seemed to have a certain predilection for treading on things which yielded under her feet and collapsed, e.g. flowers, vegetable offal, acorns, haycocks, straw and fresh hay. On our walks through the garden, on which we were usually left to ourselves, I had become used to looking on at these manœuvres, and generally scolded her for them. Now it was at that time a particular pleasure for me – and it is one in which I am still glad to indulge – to lie stretched out on a thick hearthrug in front of a good open fire. One evening I found myself in this position again, we were alone, and she went through the room to get something from the mantelpiece. Instead of stretching out her leg over me, she trod jokingly upon me, meaning to show me what she would do with hay and straw. Naturally I chimed in with the joke and laughed. After she had stood on me for some moments, she lifted up the hem of her dress and, while holding on to the cornice of the fireplace, stretched one of her elegant feet in woven silken stockings and high-heeled shoes in the shine of the fire to warm them, looking down on them the while and laughing at my heated face. She was a quite unconstrained and attractive girl, and I am pretty sure that, albeit she was visibly pleased by my excitation and the contact of my body under her foot, did not clearly understand on this first occasion in what exact condition I was. Also I don't remember that, although the desire for sexual gratification was almost driving me crazy, any comparable feeling broke to the surface in her. I seized the uplifted foot and kissed it and bore it, in an absolutely irresistible impulse, on to my erect penis. Almost at the moment her weight fell upon the latter, I had, for the first time in my life, a complete and genuine orgasm. No description can give any idea of my feelings – I only know that from that moment onwards my displaced sexual flashpoint was fixed forever. Innumerable times after that evening I felt the weight of her elegant slippers, and nothing subsequent will ever come up to the idea of the enjoyment I then experienced through her. I know that she had just as much pleasure in trampling on me as I had in being trampled. She was in a position to permit herself wide expenditure on *toilette*, and when she saw that she caused me pleasure, she went on buying lovely stockings and elegant shoes with such high and pointed heels as she could find, and then demonstrated them to me with the greatest pleasure, she standing on them, while I had to lie down and let her test them out on me. She admitted that she had great pleasure in seeing them sink into my body when she trod on it, and rejoiced in the crackling of the muscles under the heel when they moved it. After some minutes I always led her shoe on to my penis, and she would tread carefully albeit with all her weight, some fifty-five kilograms, upon me and would gaze upon me with shining eyes, with reddened cheeks, quivering lips when she, as clearly must have been the case, perceived the throb of my penis under her foot, whereon ejaculation followed. I have not the slightest doubt that she had an orgasm at the same time, although we never spoke of it. This happened over the course of several years on every favourable opportunity we had, and after a month or two of separation, four or five times every day. Sometimes I used to masturbate in her absence, by pressing with her shoe on my penis as hard as I could, imagining the while that it was she who trod me. My pleasure in this, of course, was a good deal weaker. We never mentioned ordinary sexual intercourse, and we were both well contented and let things go their way. When I was something over twenty years old I went off travelling, and on returning three years later found her married. Although we often used to see each other, no allusion to that matter was ever made, but we remained good friends. I admit that I often then looked at her feet, when no one could notice, and would gladly have accepted the pleasure which she could have bestowed upon me by occasional resumption of our remarkable practices. But it never came to that.

'Then I went off travelling again. Now she and her husband are dead. From time to time I have casual relations with prostitutes, always in the way which we have had under contemplation. I prefer a lady of my own class or of higher class willing to trample on me. But that is remarkably difficult to contrive.

'From the hundred or so women (who according to my estimate have trod on me at home or abroad) I can affirm that eighty to eighty-five were not prostitutes. At the outside, ten to twelve of them experienced sexual excitation, but if they openly showed excitement, they did not obtain satisfaction. So far as I know, that young girl was the only one to get complete sexual rapture. I have never spent many words in asking a woman to tread upon me to gratify me sexually (prostitutes apart) but have always sought to bring this about in a joking or teasing manner, and it is very dubious whether more than a few married women really knew, even if they had given me the most extreme pleasure, that they had in fact done so, since my excitement and my movements under their feet could equally well be attributed to the trampling with which they favoured me. Certainly, many of them understood what was afoot (and most of them only did it once), and although neither they nor I ever spoke of it, they were not disinclined to trample on me as much as I demanded. I do not believe that they themselves had sexual pleasure in it, although they could openly see that I did, and they did not refuse to accord it to me. I have with many women spent longer than a year in urging them to accede at last to my wishes – and have often ended by attaining what I wanted, but more often it has not come off. I never risk it until I am certain that I am going to succeed in my demand, and I have never had to endure a single serious rejection. In very many cases I can say that the acceding to my demand by the woman in question has been regarded as humouring a disingenuous and perhaps ludicrous whim, wherein there was little beyond the novelty of treading on a man to attract her. Exactly as in the case of normal seduction, the attempt to move the woman to do what I want without evoking her resistance is a great part of the charm for me, and the higher the social class to which she belongs, the harder it is, and all the more attractive. I have found that three prostitutes had performed this service to other men and were perfectly well informed about the whole business. It is not without interest that all three of these women were of lovely strong bodily build – the one of them two hundred centimetres tall and weighing almost eighty-five kilograms – but had peculiarly unmoving faces. The weight, the body structure and the clothing also excite me very strongly all at the same time. I find that a sudden prod at the extreme instant of sexual enjoyment is capable of heightening and prolonging the latter. My physical pleasure depends upon the circumstance that when the woman stands with all her weight upon my penis held between her foot and the yielding substratum of my own abdomen, the ejaculation and the orgasm last an extraordinarily long time. It is for this reason that I have the greatest preference for half-shoes with high heels. The sperm has to be squeezed through two different obstacles – one due to the tight pressure of the heel on the root of the penis; the other due to pressure by the ball of the foot, which laces the upper half together; between them there is only left free the piece under the vaulted sole of the shoe. The enjoyment is greatly heightened by urine retention, and for that reason I always try to keep back as much urine as possible.'

This case is virtually self-explanatory, for it would be difficult to imagine a more lucid account of the feelings experienced by the shoe fetishist, and the reader will be by now sufficiently familiar with the way in which discovery of the fetish object is linked with the first experience of orgasm to comprehend the genesis of this case. Let us, instead, contrast it with a case which has no such overt connections with masochism.

Shoes have always fascinated Howard T. At first he thought them merely pretty and even as a child glanced first at a woman's shoes, taking a violent dislike to ugly or clumsy ones. At the age of about twelve, he began to masturbate frequently and noticed that he often became aroused when cleaning his mother's and sisters' shoes, a chore which had been assigned him by his father. His excitement came not only from the visual contemplation of the shoes, but from the odour of stale sweat which they frequently held. Sniffing a pair of shoes while cleaning them gave him his first conscious experience of involuntary ejaculation, although he had experienced orgasm before as the result of deliberate penile manipulation.

'After that, I noticed shoes more and more. I began to borrow my sisters' and sometimes my mother's shoes and would press my penis into them. I sniffed them, rubbed them against my naked body and even tried to insert the heels into my anus. I frequently ejaculated inside them and over them.'

Howard T has never lost his adoration of shoes, but his masochism is very latent. He seeks only to caress and smell the shoes, and likes to copulate with a woman wearing high heels. He does not, however, seek to be trodden on or abused in any way. He simply likes to be able to see shoes during the sexual act and to have them as masturbation objects when no woman is available to him. A similar case which has more overtly masochistic connotations concerns Robert P who says:

'I like to have a woman sit on the edge of a bed in stockings and high heels. I kneel before her and run my hands over her sheer nylons and dainty feet. I kiss her shoes before removing them, smell them and her feet, and then, later, having taken off her stockings, I love to lick and kiss and even to suck her toes.'

In this instance the idea of adoration is clearly stated, but apart from his posture and signs of worship, Robert P does not seek to experience pain. Yet he takes pleasure in an act which would be repugnant to most men, thus proving Krafft-Ebing's contention that shoe fetishism and masochism are inextricably linked.

Perhaps because there appears to be a strong element of masochism in the female psychological make-up, a number of cases have been recorded of women who have had a definite fetishistic involvement with boots. Here again the psychological implications are extremely important. The boots transmit the idea of a powerful masculinity which strongly appeals to most women without there being any overt evidence of masochism. Indeed, as in this case, reported by Krafft-Ebing, the symbolism of the boot is totally exclusive.

'This concerns the daughter of a general who from her youth displayed a particular passion for her father's shiny riding boots. "A man on horseback in top-boots is really what I call a proper man." She rejected sundry wooers and got engaged to a lieutenant-colonel about thirty years old. She rebutted all the objections advanced by her family by adverting to his delicious feet [riding boots]. She is fatally enamoured by his magnificent riding boots. A civilian with low "sloppy" shoes is no man to her. "In front of riding boots one can tremble and at the same time adore them." Naturally the marriage was unsuccessful. Probably she is sexually anaesthetic. She advised a girl-friend not to marry on the grounds that naked feet were frightful. "A man with naked feet is a horror. If I only imagine to myself a big toe, it gives me the shudders, and the nails, which are always crippled, and the little toes which cannot grow, all that is a grisly sight!" She herself liked to wear boots reaching up as high as possible, because of the stiff appearance and the pleasant sensation of being laced in. "High boots are deliciously becoming, because they cover up the shapes of the lower calf, while leather gaiters and elastic supports let them stand out in an unsuitably sharp manner."

'As a child she had yearned for high riding boots for herself and had been happy when her father gave her high riding boots for a birthday present.'

It is quite clear from this that not even the masculine foot has any meaning for the girl. The symbolic value of the boots is entirely concerned with an ideal of masculinity which bears little relation to reality and none at all to the practicalities of married life. Other women, however, have had a much more obvious masochistic involvement with men's footwear, as the following case, cited by one of Krafft-Ebing's followers, reveals.

'The patient, Miss Y, was twenty-nine, a schoolmistress, of normal physical development but highly nervous. She was easily moved to tears and loath to punish her pupils. She was the subject of scandal in the small town of C . . . where her uncontrollable impulses had led her into questionable behaviour with senior male pupils.

'The patient believed that a woman's role was necessarily subservient to that of the masculine sex. Her vocation, however, necessitated that she maintain discipline and even punish boys for their misdemeanours. This preyed upon her mind and she believed that by punishing her male charges she was implanting a false idea of the natural relation of the sexes in their minds. She would therefore, after having administered the cane, prostrate herself before the "wronged" pupil and beseech his forgiveness. Crawling on her stomach she would kiss and caress his dusty, heavy boots and would beseech the chastised boy to trample upon her, to assert his natural masculinity and so redress the balance which, she maintained, had been falsely upset by the demands of her profession.'

However, women feature most strongly in cases of shoe and boot fetishism as the active or sadistic partners. Their role is encouraged and even assigned to them by men, but it is not entirely without its attractions. Mrs L is married to a man who delights in masochistic self-debasement. At first this came as a considerable shock to her, but she quickly realized that without some act of adoration connected with her footwear, Mr L was impotent. The more she lived up to his ideal of the dominant woman, the greater was his virility and, as Mrs L admitted, this role playing assumed, with time, a definite sexual meaning for her.

'By and large, women are so indoctrinated from birth with the idea that they must serve and care selflessly for their menfolk, that I don't think any woman, if she is really honest, can resist the opportunity to have the upper hand from time to time, and if a happy sex life is dependent upon it, then a woman who refuses is a fool.

'I now find it very exciting. Often I prepare for my husband coming home well in advance and these preparations genuinely excite me. First I have a nice hot bath, which thoroughly relaxes me. Then I put on black undies, a cut-away bra, brief pants and suspender belt with long black suspenders which I fasten to black nylons. What really gets me, though, is pulling on my special red leather boots. They reach way up my thighs, are very tight and have four-inch spiked heels. Even I can see that I look pretty exciting in them, and the moment my husband sees me dressed like that, he drops to his knees and begs to be allowed to lick and kiss my feet.

'No woman can really resist the idea of adoration. She *likes* to be worshipped, to be an omnipotent goddess for a few hours. That somehow makes her final sexual capitulation to the male even more rewarding and enjoyable.'

The boots which Mrs L wears for her husband's delectation excite her because she connects them mentally with the sexual pleasure to which they are a necessary preliminary. It is the knowledge of what they foreshadow and not the boots themselves which excite her. In fact, she is not a boot fetishist at all, in the accepted definition of the term, but her husband most certainly is.

'The moment I see her in her boots, I feel deliciously weak, like a child who can put everything else out of his mind and earn the pleasure other men take for granted. I like to lie at her feet and caress her boots. I get excited at once. I kiss them, fondle her calves and raise up the booted foot to suck the spiked heel. It is my way of proving my love, and to know that I am in her power, that at any moment she can kick or trample on me only increases my pleasure. When she was in hospital once, I used to take her boots to bed with me and cuddle them all night. That excited me terribly.'

Even the fetishist who does not connect a pair of shoes or boots with a specific woman likes to imagine that they are worn by some powerful female figure. The addiction is so strong and the masochistic element so universal that a perfectly innocent woman, utterly non-sadistic, will seem like a dominant virago to the boot fetishist. He will not be aware of anything else. A completely unknown girl, wearing boots, will be enough to fire his imagination and lead him into exotic fantasies which delight and absorb him. The message of the boots is so strong that it is inconceivable to him that a woman wearing them is not a cruel, remote goddess whose natural role is to be worshipped by him.

It is this aspect of boot and shoe fetishism which most commonly occupies the writers of erotica. There have been, of course, books built around the charm of these objects alone, but it is much more usual for them to be allied to stories of cruelty and sadism, with the woman playing the dominant role. For example :

'The tiled floor was cold against his naked body, yet he welcomed the chill which penetrated his flesh. How long had he been lying there? He had no idea, could not even tell from the degree of pain in his clenched, immobile muscles. It did not matter anyway. Each second only increased his sense of delicious anticipation. A hundred times he had imagined how it would be and then, at last, he heard the infinitely exciting click-click of approaching heels. He shivered with dread and excitement. He dared not raise his head, but at last, just when the sound of high heels on the tiles seemed to be unbearably loud, he saw the sharp-pointed toes of her boots, a bright, dazzling green with six-inch high heels, stop before him. Her legs were planted astride, and the supple green leather moulded to her fine ankles and accentuated the erotic swelling of her calves.

' "Well?" she rasped. "Aren't you going to greet me?"

'He tried to nod, bashing his chin against the tiles. His

throat was too dry and constricted with excitement to permit him to speak. He inched forward, closer, closer until she disdainfully extended one foot towards him. Propping himself up on his numbed elbows, he caught it reverently, his finger-tips thrilling to the contact of soft leather. He kissed the extended toe, filling his kiss with all the passion he felt but dare not express. He turned the foot slightly. It was so small, so elegant. How he loved it! Extending his tongue, he licked the sharp point of the heel and since she did not complain, took it all into his mouth, revelling in its hardness on his tongue, in the smell of polished leather which filled his nostrils. His body felt warm now, achingly warm, longing to spill its juices on her beautiful boots. He shuddered at the thought, and obediently released the foot she jerked impatiently away from him.

'His hands touched her ankle and kneeling, little by little, his knees bruised by the cold, hard tiles, he inched his way up, pressing each inch of her leather-covered leg with his lips, murmuring low sounds of passion. Up and up, past the shapely green ball of the knee, to the firm thigh, so tightly gripped by green leather until her own pungent scent mingled with the subtle perfume of the leather.

'He sighed, clutched her tighter. She poked with her booted foot between his thighs.

' "Shall I step on it? Nasty thing! Shall I?"

' "Yes, yes," he cried, in an agony of ecstasy, and rolled over on to his side, placing it, swollen and twitching, beside her foot. She raised the ball of her foot from the ground, pivoting it on the spiked heel, and laughed softly.'

The popularity of boots and shoes as fetish objects is obviously influenced by their perennial necessity and the fact that they, unlike underwear, for example, are always visible, always accessible. They are an essential part of clothing, primarily more functional than decorative, but fashion has turned them into a major part of a woman's wardrobe. They are an excellent example of the way in which the needs of comfort and the desire for beauty have combined to make a ready sexual substitute for many men. Yet it is man himself who has endowed these harmless objects with emotional connotations which have, as we have seen, in turn enslaved him. Boots and shoes are now so closely and so universally identified with the bizarre sexuality of sado-masochism that it would be pointless to pretend that they will not continue to exert a strange fascination on many men. At present, boots and shoes are clumsy and inelegant in design. From this we can safely predict a swing to lighter, more elegant styles in the near future. But this will not decrease the shoes' erotic value. The message of sadistic domination will simply be replaced by symbols of delicate femininity which will undoubtedly find their admirers, as long as man continues to take pleasure in making himself lesser, more vulnerable, in the act of physical worship.

PART TWO: MATERIAL FETISHISM

5: Introduction

CLOTHING is made of various materials and, as we have seen, the particular attributes of the fabric play a part in the fetishist's devotion to the specific article of clothing. But our second group of fetish objects are made up exclusively of materials. In discussing underclothing, we saw that it was the article which primarily mattered and not the stuff of which it was made. That played only a small, subsidiary role in the addiction. Material fetishists, however, are interested in the substance and in the majority of cases the way in which the material is made up is of very secondary importance indeed. To the material fetishist a remnant or bolt of the chosen material is just as erotic as a garment made out of it. Of course, he will like to dress, or to have others dress, in the favoured material, but he might equally well choose to cover his walls in it, or just to keep a fragment of it by him. For example, if his addiction is to silk, then he is just as likely to express this by sleeping between silk sheets as to wear silk shirts. This does not mean that he is a sheet fetishist, but that he simply seeks as many opportunities as possible to be in contact with his fetish object.

In one sense material fetishism is less direct, less specific, than clothing fetishism. It seldom conjures up images of a specific or even idealized woman but provides a general aura of sexuality. Inevitably, if the material is worn, the fetishist tends to seek garments fashioned from the material that bring it into close contact with the genitals, but it is perfectly possible for him to be equally excited by simply feeling a fragment of the material.

As we would expect, the charm of a certain material is about equally compounded of its physical and its emotive properties. Its look, feel and smell all entrance the fetishist but a great deal of influence is also exerted by the material's connotations, or the 'message' it gives him. As always this 'message' tends to be universal in that a large number of people are aware of the same connotations from one particular substance. With time, certain materials have taken on a specific aura which is definable but difficult to comprehend for those who persist in regarding them as mere, lifeless fabrics. This aura is compounded both of the material's natural associations and those which have accrued to it as a result of common usage.

For example, leather, which is undoubtedly the most common fetish material, has general connotations of toughness and masculinity. Physically it resembles the skin and, as everyone knows, it originally was the skin of an animal. Thus it is the material closest to the human body, with strong animal connotations. And until it was adopted by fashion designers it was associated through usage with riding, military life and power figures in general. Its message of sadistic masculinity takes on new ambivalent meanings when it is worn by a woman. Similarly, rubber, another very common fetish substance, has connotations of childhood, via aprons, waterproof pants, toys, etc., and of medical practice via enemas, rubber tubing,* etc. These

* See *The Kinky Crowd* by Clavel Brand, Luxor Press, 1970, for a complete examination of rubber and leather fetishism. Also *The Leather Scene* by Roger Farley-Gray, Canova Press, 1969, a pictorial examination of the fascination of leather.

connotations, which are aided and abetted by the physical appearance of the material, enable it to act as an agent, via which the fetishist is able to re-create and recapture a world, a time, which has otherwise vanished.

Invariably the addiction to a certain material as a sexual substitute is fixed by early orgasm association. Thereafter the material becomes essential to the achievement of orgasm because it is mentally regarded as a part of the whole pleasurable process. Indeed, association is the key to fetishism. Sexual pleasure is associated with the material. Its feel, odour, visual appearance as associated with specific experiences, memories and images. The material itself is associated with ideas and concepts which are, for various reasons, sexually exciting to the fetishist. Thus the material is an agent which enables the fetishist to reach his particular and idiosyncratic sexual universe. It is the intermediary between him and the realization of sexual expression. His body and mind rejoice in the material, just as the average man rejoices in the presence of a loved and desired woman. The material stands in place of the woman and is preferred to her.

As Krafft-Ebing pointed out, one of the most important aspects determining fetishism is the patient's attitude to sexual intercourse. He is invariably indifferent, or at least dependent upon the presence of the material. But the fetishist, if faced with a choice between sexual intercourse and private indulgence with his favoured object, would undoubtedly choose the latter. 'For it is an absolute and essential part of fetishism that the ejaculation, the orgasm, should not be attained through the normal act of sex, but either through masturbation (wherein quite often the most remarkable methods of friction will be used) or – less often – without sensible stimulation, by mental means' (Krafft-

93

Ebing). This indifference may be caused by some psychological trauma connected with the proper partner which results in aversion, but most commonly fetishism is the direct result of misplaced sexual focus, which results more in a preference for the substitute than an active dislike of coitus.

Material fetishism, then, strongly resembles other forms of the aberration in both its motives and causes. It does tend, however, to be vaguer, to deal in more general terms and to have an even less obvious sexual meaning than even gloves or shoes. To comprehend the attraction, however, is simply a matter of accepting the misplaced sexual focus, to understand and accept that the object occupies the place and function of the partner, save that it is completely passive.

6: Fur

AT the time of writing his *Psychopathia Sexualis*, Krafft-Ebing considered fur to be the most common material singled out for fetishistic usage. Second he placed velvet, and then silk. Today we have no hesitation in placing these materials lower down the list. Leather and rubber are certainly the most common, or popular, fetish materials today. To this extent, material fetishism is influenced by fashion and current trends. During Krafft-Ebing's lifetime fur was a much more common human covering, while leather was considered as a workaday material fit only for the working classes. Velvet was common for ladies' gowns and men's frock coats, but today it is considered too fragile and expensive a material for everyday use in these less leisured times. Climate, too, of course plays a part in the 'popularity' of a fetish material. In hot or tropical climates fur is, obviously, unnecessary and therefore scarce. Consequently few fur fetishists will be found among the inhabitants of countries which enjoy a hot climate. But in the cold winters of Europe it is a popular and ideal means of warmth and protection. However, leather and rubber have been so well documented that we will concentrate on the comparatively more unusual fur and velvet.

Most people enjoy the feel of soft fur. The long pelt possesses a silky quality which is, in itself, pleasant and most of us will have experienced the tickling sensation which results when the hand is run lightly over a fur coat. The softness of fur attracts a great many people. Small children are often drawn to animals, to furry toys, and their mothers' fur coats, exactly because of this soft warmth which is naturally pleasing. It has even been suggested that our unique nakedness attracts us to the pelts of animals as a sort of compensation process. Although unfounded and unlikely. this idea is lent some credence by the fact that it is a common occurrence for men and women to profess envy of the animals for their warm, natural fur coats. What is certainly true is that fur possesses very definite animal connotations. These are, in fact, even more easily comprehended than the similar connotations of leather. Fur remains recognizably the pelt of an animal and no attempt is ever made to disguise the fact. Thus, in one sense, when a woman wears a leopard-skin coat, she is dressing up as a leopardess. Yet the softness and beauty of the pelt is in direct contrast to the obvious images of fleetness, strength, and virility, of animals which fur tends to conjure up. It is this physical softness and erogenous silkiness which distinguishes the attraction of fur from that of leather. The latter is invariably connected, for the fetishist, with sadism, whereas fur's very softness seems to inspire a luxurious gentleness in its devotees.

Nor should we overlook the fact that, despite its one-time universal accessibility, fur has been, for many years now, an extremely expensive material. It is true that in the last five years, fur has been placed within the reach of the majority, but it still retains an air of luxury and expensiveness. For over a century, fur was reserved, by virtue of its price, for the rich. To many people a fur coat was the very height of luxury, a garment to which they could only aspire and which was associated in their minds with the rich, aristocratic and unattainable ladies they glimpsed from a distance. This tends to lend fur a spurious glamour, an element of exoticism which, as we shall endeavour to demonstrate in the following pages, has been influential in some cases of fur fetishism. Now that fur coats have become so much cheaper and more plentiful, now that almost any woman can possess one, it is likely that this aspect of the fetish will disappear, just as the sudden popularity of fur coats for men will probably result, in time, in a new increase in female and homosexual cases of fur fetishism.

Fur rugs and displayed animal hides have always been a mark of opulence. For many people they are associated with the fearless archetypal image of the ultra-masculine big-game hunter. Like the specifically animalistic connotations, this human element is connected with adventure and bravery, a sort of idealized masculinity which stretches back, of course, to man's earliest roots when he was, by definition and necessity, a hunter. So much of human sexual practice is a ritualistic attempt to redress the balance of civilization, to reach back to man's prime, uncomplicated role, that this aspect of fur fetishism should not be dismissed. Civilization has tended to confine sex, to make it seem unnatural and reprehensible, which is in direct conflict with our natural instincts. One of the most important and persuasive aspects of fetishism of many kinds is its ability to reassert this original, natural attitude to the whole concept of sex. It is, of course, an instinctive element and not a deliberate one, but it can be argued that its importance is all the greater because of this.

Important as these mental connotations of a material are, when they are used as fetish objects, it is dangerous to be too explicit about them, for they are very frequently only unconsciously perceived. Few fetishists are able to verbalize about them, and it is salutary to remember that, in the early days of psychological research, Krafft-Ebing insisted that material fetishism was determined solely by tactile stimuli. The importance of mental connotations is still imperfectly understood and they obviously have a much more general application than any concrete revelations they make about individual cases. But even before this aspect of fetishism was considered, it was implicit in the statements of devotees, like the following which was recorded by Krafft-Ebing himself.

'From my earliest youth I had a deeply rooted craze for furs and velvet, peculiar in the sense that these stuffs produce a sexual excitation in me, the sight and touch of them move me to pleasurable delight. I am unable to recall any particular event such as the appearance of my first sexual excitation simultaneously with the impression produced by these stuffs, for instance, first being excited by a woman

97

who was dressed in it, nor even generally how this enthusiasm of mine first began.

'I only know that even as a tiny child I was always keenly straining to see and stroke furs, and got a dark sensation of pleasure from it. When definite conceptions of a sexual nature first occurred to me, I mean the intention of sexual thought on to a woman, there already existed a curious preference for a woman dressed in precisely that kind of material.

'And so it has remained right up to my years of mature manhood. A woman wearing furs or velvet, or indeed both, excites me far more quickly and violently than one not clothed in this way. The stuffs in question are not the unconditional prerequisite of excitation; desire responds to the normal stimuli even without them, but the sight and particularly the touch of these fetish materials constitute for me a potent reinforcement of other normal charms and an enhancement of the erotic enjoyment. Often the very sight of even an only passably pretty woman, provided she be dressed in this stuff, lifts me into lively excitement and quite transports me. Incidentally, the penetrating smell of fur is quite indifferent to me then, if anything it is unpleasing and only tolerable by reason of the association with pleasant visual and tactile sensations. I yearn strongly to feel these materials on a woman's body, to stroke them, kiss them, bury my face in them. My highest pleasure is to see and feel my fetish on a woman's shoulder.

'Fur alone or velvet alone exert on me the effect I have described, the former far more potently than the latter. The strongest of all is a combination of them both. Even articles of female clothing when seen and felt alone without the owner, have a sexually exciting effect upon me and also – albeit in a lesser degree – fur worked up into rugs and thus no part of female attire, as also velvet or plush when used on furniture or draperies . . . The very word "fur" has to me a magical quality and at once evokes erotic imagination.

'Fur only has the effect described on me when it has thick, fine, smooth, pretty long and outstanding hairs of the type called "whisker-hairs". It is on these, as I have quite clearly observed, that the effect depends. I am perfectly indifferent to not only the coarse, tufty kinds of fur which are generally considered ordinary, but also to those considered beautiful and noble, in which the whisker-hair is far apart (seals, beaver) or short by nature (as ermine) or unduly long and supine (apes, bears). The specific effect is only produced by the standing whisker-hairs of sables, martens, skunks and suchlike . . . The effect seems in fact to depend on a quite definite impression of thick, fine hair-tips on the end organs of the sensitive nerves.'

There is no mistaking the fact that this man is aware of the animal connotations of fur, although he does not elucidate on the point. As always with Krafft-Ebing, this is a classic case, illustrated by a very dispassionate assessment of the fetish substance's attraction. It is, as we see, allied specifically to women and to their clothing and from this we may be permitted to assume that his sexual response to the tactile stimulation of fur is aided and abetted by his close association of the material with women. The tactile stimuli were probably augmented by mental images of some desirable woman. In this sense, fur acts as an agent or substitute for a real partner and its true erotic meaning, apart from its exciting feel, may be adduced to its association, apparently unexplained, in the patient's mind with women.

A far more complex case is that which concerns Gerald

F. At forty-three Gerald F is a confirmed bachelor and a reasonably successful business executive. He has been careful with his money and now lives very comfortably. Anyone visiting his home would find it unremarkable, in all probability, except for the large bedroom. The floor of this dark, sparsely furnished room is covered with a fitted carpet of long, black, slightly curling fur. The large bed is made of a low, mattress-covered dais on which are an assortment of fur rugs and fur-covered pillows. The walls are covered in heavy flock paper and there is even a heavy fur curtain which covers the window. In a corner cupboard more, smaller, fur rugs are kept and even a cursory examination of these will reveal that they are stained and dirty. The ceiling of the room is covered with mirror tiles. In this room, Gerald F enacts a strange, solitary ritual.

'Before I enter the room, whether it is for one of my fur sessions or just to go to bed, I always take off my shoes and socks and leave them outside the door. Then, the moment I step on to the carpet my feet sink into luxuriant fur. That is a sensation I can scarcely describe. It's partly like being pleasantly tickled and partly a gorgeous feeling of having one's feet buried in soft, yielding fur. I undress slowly, putting each of my garments away in turn. I hate to have anything lying about to distract from the impression of being surrounded by fur. By the time I'm nude the sensation of fur on my feet and the general anticipation will have excited me. Then I lie down on the floor, or on the bed, and move my body against the fur. It is like being brushed by a thousand tiny feelers and my whole body seems to be turned into a receptacle for sensual pleasure. My backside, my thighs, my belly and chest, every part of me responds to these fur-induced sensations.

'Sometimes I keep this up for hours. More and more I

bring my erect penis into contact with the fur and, at last, when I can stand it no longer, I get one of the small rugs out and lie upon it, forcing my penis into it and moving my hips up and down until I reach a shattering orgasm. Because of the mess I have special fur rugs for this climax to my sessions.'

In response to further questions, Gerald F said:

'No, I don't think of anything specific during these periods of sensual abandon, but in a curious way the fur is the woman. I can't express it any more clearly than that. I suppose in a way the soft silky touch of long fur is my idea of what a woman should feel like. I know that on the few occasions when I have been with a woman, I am disappointed by the feel of her flesh. Neither it nor the idea of copulation appeals to me nearly as much as covering my naked body with the tantalizing caress of fur.

'Why do I do it? I don't know, really, I mean, there's no simple answer. Because I like to, I suppose. It's my way of having sex. I get my pleasure in this way as opposed to the more "normal" one. It's simply a question of understanding that when I'm rolling about naked on a lot of fur rugs, I am intensely excited and reach orgasm without ever touching myself. I sometimes think that to me, fur is the essence of femininity with which I can, whenever I choose, completely surround myself.'

One of Gerald F's earliest memories is of being held on the lap of a woman wearing a fur coat. He clearly recalls that the woman, whose identity he cannot recall, laid her hand on his bare thigh and absent-mindedly caressed his leg as she conducted a conversation with his mother.

'I remember being diffused by a warm glow and dimly perceiving distinctly pleasurable sensations. I laid my cheek against her fur-covered breast. It was so soft and warm, so gentle against my skin. That and the rhythmic movement of her hand on my leg induced in me feelings of complete safety and security. I never wanted to move from her lap. I nearly went to sleep when she held me and I remember crying when she put me down and stood up to go. Ever since that day, fur in any form has exercised an uncontrollable hold on me.'

This remark about feelings of safety and security is undoubtedly the clue to Gerald F's fetishistic involvement with fur. His lack of interest in women, which persists despite very strong and entirely heterosexual impulses, indicates that he is afraid of women and uses fur as a substitute because it provides him with sensations of security. His childhood was an extremely unhappy one and he had a very contradictory relationship with his mother who, for various reasons, had very little time for him. The memory of the woman in the fur coat is, in fact, one of the few pleasant memories he has of his early years. In that memory are centred his association of sex with women and of material comfort. Now he finds both through the agency of fur rugs and carpets. He cocoons himself in them, using them as a symbolic protection against his mother's indifference and rejection, and associating them with sex which he fears to share with women in case he is again rejected. Significantly he says, 'I sometimes think that if I could meet the woman in the fur coat I could fall in love with her and do anything for her.' The very unattainability of this woman acts as a barrier between him and available women and increases his dependence upon fur which gives him all the things he lacked as a child as well as a fear-free means of sexual release.

A case of fur fetishism which arose through the trauma of unrequited love was recorded a few years ago. It is an extremely sad case which has an unusual element of social comment in it. As a young man, Wilfred C worked as an under-gardener on a large estate owned by a rich and well-connected family. His father and mother had both worked for the family and as a child Wilfred and his sisters had played with the children from the 'big house'. He had always enjoyed a rather special relationship with the youngest daughter which was interrupted by her being sent to a finishing school for several years. She returned to the estate a beautiful and poised young woman. Wilfred saw her from time to time and she occasionally stopped to talk to him in the garden. Wilfred fell completely in love with the young woman and began to live solely for a glimpse of her or a few words with her. When one day she dropped a fur-lined glove in the garden, Wilfred put it in his pocket instead of returning it to her. There was nothing sinister in this. He merely wanted a keepsake of the girl he loved. He did not use the glove for any sexual purpose, but fondled it while daydreaming about her. He later claimed that he came to associate the soft feel of the glove's fur lining with the girl.

Eventually, Wilfred heard that the girl was going away again and he summoned up the courage to confess his love. The girl was undoubtedly shocked. What seemed to Wilfred perfectly normal and natural struck her as impossible. With her superior poise and social manner, she laughingly dismissed the idea as preposterous and told the love-lorn Wilfred not to be silly. Wilfred was deeply pained. It had not occurred to him that his childhood friend would not return his affection and that night, as an act of revenge for her cruelty, he destroyed the glove he had so carefully treasured, during which act he became very excited sexually and experienced an involuntary orgasm.

Soon after this, Wilfred left the estate and for a time drifted from job to job. He was restless and seemed unable to settle. Once he was arrested for assault, but the case was dismissed when it was understood that he had merely stroked the back of a woman's fur coat in a crowded shop. His defence was that he had been so attracted by the beauty of the coat that he had unthinkingly touched it. The court was satisfied that there was no intent to commit an assault, but what they did not know was that the fur coat was, as far as Wilfred C was concerned, a symbol of the girl who had rejected him and that even momentary contact with it had given him an erection.

After the case, he moved to a larger town and took a job there as a doorman/cloakroom attendant at an exclusive social club which was predominantly patronized by the wealthy. Some time after his arrival the management began to receive complaints from various members that something had been spilt on their fur coats when they left them in the cloakroom. Wilfred was questioned about this but denied all knowledge. However, various lady visitors to the club compared notes and the complaints continued to come in. After paying several expensive cleaning bills, the management decided to keep a close watch on the cloakroom in the hope of solving the mystery. The following statement, made by the manager of the club and corroborated by two other witnesses, was read in court.

'I kept watch for some time and about nine o'clock, after most of the guests had arrived, I observed the defendant moving along the rows of deposited coats stroking and examining all the ladies' fur coats. No others seemed to interest him, although he did examine the fur collar of a woman's tweed coat for a moment or two. After a time, he chose one fur coat and carried it to the back of the room where he hung it on the wall. The defendant then unbuttoned his trousers and pulled out his erect organ which he pressed against the fur coat. He began to make copulatory movements against the coat and swiftly ejaculated over it.'

Wilfred C was, in fact, caught red-handed. As a result of this evidence he was referred to a psychiatrist and, on his report, was placed in a mental hospital for some time. During the investigation of his case, two significant facts came to light. One was that Wilfred had never had intercourse with a woman and the other that the girl he had loved had frequently worn an expensive fur coat. Wilfred believed, with, of course, some degree of accuracy, that the young woman had rejected him upon purely social grounds. He had been rejected because he was not good enough for her. This increased the natural hurt he felt at having his love spurned and the act of destroying her glove was a symbolic revenge which had also excited him sexually. Because of this association between fur and sexual excitement, he saw fur coats as a symbol of both the remote, cruel women who were, socially, out of his reach and as a means of attaining sexual fulfilment. He polluted as many fur coats as he could in order to revenge himself against a class of women whom he believed despised and rejected him as a man. Yet no other sort of woman attracted him at all. He was indifferent to working-class girls but drawn to and excited by rich, well-groomed women in fur coats. During the course of investigation he revealed the following fantasy.

'Whenever I did what I did on a fur coat, I always used to imagine that the woman who owned it would discover me. She would be sickened by the sight of my ejaculation on her precious fur, but then she would get angry and, putting the coat on, would punish me.'

From this we can see that Wilfred's fetishism was strangely linked with a mixture of sado-masochistic impulses. He wanted to revenge himself for his rejection by polluting the coats, but he also then wanted to affirm his 'natural' social role by being punished by the offended women. These punishment fantasies were invariably sexually exciting. He also imagined raping a woman in a fur coat and then being beaten by her. Thus we can see that his fetish for fur coats (fur in any other form did not particularly interest him) was as much a social symbol, a mark of class, as it was a sexual one and all of his fetishistic behaviour was closely linked with a concept of social or class revenge.

Victor R first discovered the erotic power of fur via a pair of fur-lined gloves. He was an adolescent when he was given them as a Christmas present and immediately felt a pleasurable sensation when he put them on his hands. The fur lining had a considerable fascination for him and in his early masturbatory experiments he employed the gloves to heighten his sensations.

'It seemed to me perfectly logical that since I liked the feel of fur on my hands it would be even better on my very sensitive erect penis. And so, after playing with myself for a while one night, I suddenly thrust my penis into one of my gloves. It was heaven. An incredible sensation swept through me. It was as though hundreds of little tickling things were brushing against my excited flesh. I ejaculated almost at once, and used the gloves whenever I masturbated after that. It ruined them, of course, but I managed to get hold of a piece of fur which I folded around my penis and used instead.'

Victor R does not appear to be particularly highly sexed

and is apparently homosexual. He is afraid of women and does not connect them with fur. He avoids women as much as possible and has never had intercourse. He has performed mutual masturbation on infrequent occasions with other men, but he prefers another way of achieving satisfaction. He has become a successful photographer and uses his profession to help satisfy his peculiar tastes.

'My idea of a really satisfying sex act is to wear fur briefs with the fur side inside, and to photograph an attractive young man in a sexually excited state wearing a fur coat. I have several pairs of fur briefs that were made specially for me and when I put them on I immediately become excited. I can stay erect for several hours just by wearing them, but my excitement is greatly increased if I can take photographs of a semi-nude boy at the same time. I dress my models in fur boots and fur jacket, leaving their legs and genitals nude. I don't do this very often. Most of the time I like to masturbate in my fur briefs while looking at photographs of aroused men in fur coats.'

Part of the charm of these pictures lies in the impression of hirsute masculinity, of a borrowed animality symbolized by the furs. A similar attraction is experienced by a young woman, Christine P, who, although not a fur fetishist in the true sense, is certainly sexually aware of fur.

'My current boy-friend bought a fur coat last winter. I always liked the feel of it, as I do my own, but what really turned me on to it was one night when he was staying with me and had to get up to go to the lavatory and it was very cold so he put his fur coat on and when he came back he threw himself on the bed while still wearing the coat. It just made me feel terribly sexy, feeling the long fur on my breasts, and stroking it with my hands. We made love like that and since then he often wears his fur coat when we make love just because he knows I like it. He says he can tell it makes me sexier, so why not?'

Christine P is not a true fetishist because she is not dependent upon fur. She can enjoy sexual intercourse without being in contact with fur. It is simply an extra source of pleasure and in a typically female way she insists that her lover is more important than the fur coat. She merely regards it as a sexually stimulating adjunct to him. But she also claims that his wearing the fur makes him seem more aggressive, stronger and more demanding.

As with leather, these animal/masculine connotations of fur take on a very special and bizarre charm when worn by women. In erotic fiction the dominant and very desirable woman is frequently dressed in furs. The most famous example is, of course, Sacher-Masoch's celebrated *Venus in Furs** but many other books have been concerned to exploit the erotic interest of fur.

'Her arms crossed across her breasts, the collar of her fur coat turned up, he could see only her face, buried in a nest of silky fur, and the cruel red mouth twisted into a smile. Kneeling before her, he touched the soft, long-haired pelt which felt smooth and warm beneath his fingers. He moved his hands up and down the coat, following the contours of her body under its voluminous folds.

'Suddenly she let her arms fall to her sides. The coat swung open. With a strangled gasp of excitement, he realized that she was naked beneath it. Her flesh gleamed like polished marble in contrast to the thick brown fur. He laid his cheek against its soft, animal warmth, drawing in the exciting odour of it and her. She slipped the coat off one shoulder, looping the fur around and under her left

* *Venus in Furs* by Leopold von Sacher-Masoch, Luxor Press, London, 1968.

breast. It seemed doubly naked peeping pink-tipped from the surrounding fur. She pouted teasingly at him as he reached upwards, sliding his trembling hands over the ruffled fur to reach her hot breast.'

An even more overt fetishistic interest is provided in another book.

'Carmen slept between fur sheets, laid her flawless cheeks on a fur-covered pillow. Two expertly cured animal pelts were placed fur side together to form an envelope between which she slipped, gracefully naked. On top were piled a miscellaneous collection of hides, their hues and furry sheens creating the impression of opulence and erotic delight.

'The walls of the small room were covered in soft white fur, the floor with bearskins. Wherever she moved she could bring her delicious, slim body into exciting contact with the fur. She loved to be taken roughly by a strong man who forced her up against the teasing, tickling walls, where she moved her small buttocks lasciviously against the caress of what seemed to be an enormous, furry paw.'

Animal connotations reach a veritable peak in another book which describes a woman, dressed entirely in the fur of the red fox, making love with a young man dressed in snakeskin in an empty animal cage. And, of course, the symbolism of D. H. Lawrence's *The Fox*, which was recently filmed with great success, reveals a complex understanding of the erotic animal implications of fur and sexuality.

Fur fetishism is then a combination of physical and psychological stimuli which combine to attract the fetishist who uses it, as always, as a substitute for a shared sexual experience. In all but small details it parallels any other fetish object in its discovery and usage, its exclusiveness and symbolic value. People hide behind fur, or leather, rubber, etc., as an escape from the sexual realities of life for which they are ill-equipped, but, as with all sexual substitutes, what seems like a blessed release is in fact a diverting and narrowing of their natural sexual desires.

7: Velvet

VELVET is very similar to fur in so far as its prime physical appeal as a fetish substance is tactile. It has, as is well known, a very definite nap which may be described as giving a more subtle but very similar sensation to that which is perceived when fur is stroked. Its appearance is rich and luxurious and even when it was at its most popular, it was regarded as a particularly fine material, especially favoured by ladies of means for their gowns and furnishings. Today, as we have already said, velvet is still regarded as something of a luxury material but largely because of its impracticality as an everyday material and not because of its price.

Emotively, velvet speaks to the fetishist of luxury and femininity. It has, probably, less strong connotations than many other fetish materials, but this is more than balanced by the strength of its tactile appeal. This latter point is underlined in a negative way by the very large number of people who have an aversion to the feel of velvet. Be that as it may, it cannot be denied that the fetishist receives impressions of luxury and opulence from velvet and that its continued association with female clothing has also given it strong connotations of femininity.

Rightly or wrongly, materials have, over the years, been divided into roughly 'masculine' and 'feminine' groups. This categorization has been prompted by the frequency with which one or other of the sexes wears a particular material. Thus silk, satin, velvet and lace have distinctly feminine connotations, while the masculine group includes such materials as wool, tweeds, linen and leather. This grouping of materials explains why men in particular are so strongly attracted sexually to the feminine materials, but even the most cursory glance at the 'masculine' group reveals that it contains materials which can only arbitrarily be regarded as the preserve of the male. The materials most commonly associated with male clothing are also regularly worn by women. This is perhaps why there are so few women material fetishists. The materials that would naturally stand symbolically in place of the male are not at all mysterious or strange to women because their greater sartorial freedom has always enabled them to wear any material they like. It is only in recent years that men have taken over the 'feminine' materials and it is yet too early to say whether this will result in a decrease of male fetishistic interest in them.

It also raises another important question. Velvet fetishism is one of the very few areas of sexual aberration that includes a comparatively large number of female devotees, including some women who can be regarded as true fetishists. Why are they drawn to velvet? The simplest answer, of course, is that its universal adoption as a material for their clothes has increased the possibilities of their sexual exposure to it, while its very strong tactile element has increased the chances of their becoming involved with it. Indeed, so strong is the tactile appeal that a person is almost certain to have some strong response to it. But on another level it is perhaps a popular (as far as any fetish is 'popular' with women) material because it reinforces their own femininity and yet, thanks to its feel, has a greater degree of mystery than other materials. It is a unique material in so far as its appearance and feel are unique. One cannot wear or touch velvet without being aware of its peculiar feel and there is no reason to suppose that women should be any less receptive to this sensation than men.

To digress for a moment, this is a relevant place to discuss a little the baffling question of why so few women are fetishists in comparison with men. Their chances of exposure to a fetish material are equal to those of men and there is no reason to assume that their sexual focus is any less delicately balanced than the male's. Yet the fact remains that the true female fetishist is a very rare creature indeed. Accepting that women's sexual impulse is narrower, more firmly directed, than the male's, there is another purely physical aspect of the matter which is seldom taken into consideration. Fetishism is generally essential to the male as a means to erection and orgasm. Without his fetish object or substance he cannot gain an erection and without that, obviously, any real means of sexual expression is denied him. But a woman does not have any comparable physical mechanism to control before she is ready for copulation. Of course, as we know, her mental attitude is extremely important. She has, one might say, to be put in the right frame of mind for intercourse, but she is physically capable of it at any time. Therefore she does not have a comparable need for a fetish object, she is not dependent for physical readiness on anything at all. Her problems and requirements, although by no means less than a man's, are yet completely different and this goes a long way to explain why female fetishism is such a rare phenomenon.

But to revert to velvet and the fact that, in comparison with other forms of fetishism, it has a surprisingly large number of female devotees. For example, an attractive blonde called Helen K who says :

'I have made myself several pairs of velvet pants. They are velvet inside and out, are made from a double thickness of velvet, in other words. I wear these whenever I am going on a date with a man I like. By that I mean a man I think there is a chance I might go to bed with. I adore the feel of velvet, you see, and to wear it next to my skin, or rather next to my vagina, acts like some kind of foreplay. By the end of the evening I am thoroughly ready for sex. Even longing for it. I wear these pants very tight so that whenever I move, even the slightest movement, the velvet rubs against my crotch.

'If a man tries to make love to me when I've been wearing ordinary pants, it is very difficult. I get very tense and nervous about it and I'm not really ready for it at all. Of course, I can pretend, but it isn't nearly the same. I like to prepare for these things, and that means being able to wear my velvet pants for some hours before anything happens.

'I must confess that sometimes, when I haven't got a regular boy-friend, I wear my velvet pants around the house, deliberately to excite me. Then, when I go to bed, I usually masturbate by simply rubbing my pants on the outside of my vagina. But I only do that when I'm sex-starved, as you might say.'

Helen K is a true velvet fetishist. She depends upon velvet for sexual arousal. She can have intercourse without the velvet pants, but only because the female genitals are always ready, in comparison with a man's. Furthermore, she uses her velvet pants as a masturbation object. Unlike male fetishists, however, she is not indifferent to intercourse, but this is a distinction we must make in considering female fetishists. Few woman are really satisfied without complete penetration, and most prefer a man for this purpose and not a substitute. A man, on the other hand, can often be fully satisfied by self-induced orgasm. The point is that although Helen K enjoys intercourse, she does not do so without prior stimulation from velvet. She is certainly indifferent to manual stimulation by her male partner and claims that this seldom works. She likes to replace foreplay by wearing velvet and to copulate as quickly as possible once her velvet underwear is removed. Because of this important fact of penetration, Helen K makes it quite clear that masturbation is an alternative and not her favoured means of sexual expression. But when circumstances force her to masturbate, she does so with the aid of velvet.

From this we can see at once that we require slightly but importantly different criteria in assessing the female fetishist. We must not make it a condition of her addiction, as we tend to do with men, that she be indifferent or averse to intercourse. This is simply because the act of being penetrated is the essence of female sexuality. Anything else is certainly second best, while a man is capable of experiencing a true orgasm without penetrating. Thus female fetishism is likely to take the form of a means of foreplay, or arousal inducement, and not solitary masturbation. Similarly there are a number of men for whom intercourse is desirable but dependent upon their being aroused by some fetish object or material. Such cases we call ones of mild fetishism, but because of a woman's different needs, we can regard her as a true fetishist if her addiction meets the 'mild' criteria set out above.

Men and women differ in another respect with regard to fetishism. Helen K says:

'A number of my men friends have known about my passion for velvet, but they have never objected. Once they know about it they tend to ask me if I'm wearing my velvet pants. They give me presents of velvet and one man even bought himself a pair of velvet trousers. I find that they are interested in my liking for velvet. It seems to add spice to the relationship, and certainly no one has ever objected.'

We know that this attitude is in direct and dramatic contrast to that expressed by the vast majority of women when faced with a man's fetishism. Does this mean that men are more tolerant than women, or are there more complex reasons? Certainly they appear to be more tolerant, but their reaction is very largely dictated by self-interest, as is a woman's negative reaction to a man's involvement with some inanimate object or material. Men have a natural comprehension of the sexual fascination that objects and materials can exert, whereas women see themselves as the prime and even the sole object of masculine desire and source of arousal. This is, generally, true, but the path leading to the woman may be very devious indeed. Furthermore, men, given their natural acceptance of the diffuseness of sexual focus, tend to accept anything which leads to a woman's sexual compliance .They are quite happy to accept that a pair of velvet panties arouses a woman, so long as this leads to her giving herself to them, and, unlike women, they do not see the object, whatever it may be, as a rival. Men care very little about the means, and a great deal about the ends. A woman, however, faced with a man aroused by velvet feels denigrated, that she is second best. A man knows that he is not, but this only results from the different sexual needs and requirements of male and female. In the case of Helen K, her men friends undoubtedly see her fetishism as an extra source of sexual indulgence. They enjoy talking about it, even attempt to share in it, because a man is prepared to do more or less anything to increase a woman's sexual receptivity of him, while a woman invariably thinks that she alone should be stimulus enough for the male. This male attitude, of course, removes a great deal of the loneliness from female fetishism. Helen K need have no qualms about marrying, for example, for there is no shortage of men who would welcome her fetishism as an added spice to their sexual relationship. In fact, it might be argued that her popularity is increased by her fetishism, simply because of the male's attitude to it. But then the male knows that a female fetishist ultimately requires him to achieve full satisfaction, whereas a woman knows that a man is quite capable of leading a reasonably satisfying sex life without her, and so sees the fetish object as something loathsome, something to be destroyed.

Helen K's interest in velvet dates from her childhood and, in this respect, as we shall see, female fetishism parallels that of the male's in all but small and expected details.

'I come from a very working-class family and when I was a child, we children used to have to bathe every Friday night in an old zinc bath before the kitchen fire. My mother had inherited a red velvet-covered chair from some great-aunt or someone and I can clearly remember, when I was about twelve or thirteen, being sat on the chair by the fire, after being dried from the bath. Even then the contact of velvet on my bare bottom and the backs of my thighs used to send shudders through me. Without at all understanding what I was doing, I used to love to curl up in that chair and would arrange the skirt of my dress so as to bring as much of my bare legs as possible into contact with the velvet. I used to sit there and read, moving my legs all the time across the velvet seat and arms. It used to give me very pleasurable sensations, although I didn't really masturbate with the aid of the chair. But as I got older, I used to touch myself between my legs while I sat in it. Once, when I was alone in the house, I pulled my pants down, just so that I could sit with my bare buttocks on the velvet seat.

'I suppose it was because of this that I longed for a velvet party dress. Nothing else would do, and I used to worry my mother to let me have a velvet dress. She made me one eventually, and I absolutely adored it. I loved wearing it and it was the first dress I ever had that made me really conscious of myself as an attractive human being. That dress, and other velvet ones I had afterwards, seemed magic to me. I didn't see how I could fail to be pretty and attractive in a dress made of velvet. Sometimes, when I was alone, which wasn't often in a small house with three other children, I used to put my dress on inside out and without underclothes. I loved the feel of velvet next to my skin even then. And I used to wish that the dress was reversible, that the nap of the velvet could be inside and out.'

This awareness of her own desirability and femininity as a result of wearing velvet is obviously a significant factor in Helen K's velvet fetishism. It was a symbol of her sexual attractiveness, of her femininity, and since this is so important to women it is not surprising that it influenced her in her preoccupation with velvet. She feels more confident, more desirable in velvet because its feel increases her awareness of her own sensuality. Similar reactions have been recorded among male leather fetishists who, when wearing leather, claim that they feel more manly, are more aware of their sexual potential. A woman generally perceives her sexual potential through male reactions of desire, etc., but, of course, they dress deliberately to accentuate their natural attractions and velvet, because it makes her feel sexual, is the most potent symbol of this kind to Helen K. The velvet panties that she wears not only arouse her by their contact, but this arousal also makes it easier for her to believe that men will respond to her attractiveness. She is rarely disappointed.

An even more extreme case, one which apparently confirms Krafft-Ebing's dictum that a fetishist is not a true fetishist unless he or she is indifferent to intercourse, is not surprisingly, recounted, though was not originally recorded, by Krafft-Ebing himself. There can be no doubt that this 'woman, twenty-five years of age' was a genuine velvet fetishist, but similarly there is no doubt that hers was an unusually extreme case.

'The awakening of the sexual impulse is dated by the patient from her eighteenth year, when her menses began, that is to say comparatively late. Soon afterwards she took to masturbation, using her finger first of all. The patient did not observe any bodily damage arising from this. One day she discovered in herself a peculiar predilection for velvet. She found, as she expresses it, a great joy and fell into temptation on being haunted by velvety materials. She partly regretted and partly felt happy at not being employed in the velvet store section of the warehouse in which she worked. Her idea was that if she had indeed been occupied there, she would have been driven to steal velvet and thus her perversion would have come to the light of day.

'She conducted ladies of her acquaintance who came

clad in velvet over the clothes, and experienced pleasure in so doing. One day the thought went through her head, how lovely it would be to masturbate with the aid of velvet. She therefore feigned a malady some days before the beginning of her period, laid down in bed and masturbated with the aid of velvet.

'All these events took place in her eighteenth year and since then the impulse has merely increased. She especially was overpowered by it before her periods, without those near her ever coming upon the traces of it. She then feels an intense itching sensation in the genitals and a pronounced feeling of heat and these keep driving her to masturbate again and again. For normal coitus she has no feeling at all, on the contrary, she depicts marriage as a means for attaining her sexual desires in the matter of the purchase of clothes made of velvet.

'She was married at the desire of her parents. Normal coitus brought her no pleasure, it was far more a case of her yielding to her husband's urging. When arranging the furnishing of her home, she managed to contrive that the bedroom should be decorated in velvet. The bedcover too was, at her desire, made of velvet. People paid no further attention to this bizarre taste, but met the young wife's wishes. For her it meant the supreme pleasure of being able to hide herself alone in the midst of this world of velvet and labour at masturbation. She did not use the velvet bedcover for the purpose for fear of leaving stains on it from her masturbatory activities. Also, she always draped herself in velvet now. One day she had a pleasurable dream wherein she fancied herself quite naked in velvet. The dream never recurred. As a result of it she came to admit that her husband would more attract her sexually if he were to don velvet clothes, even were it only e.g. the corduroys etc. of timber workers. She declares that the imagination of her husband dressed in velvet would increase her sexual excitation in normal coitus. She is convinced that she would detect even more pleasure in that than in masturbating with velvet. She returned a negative answer to the direct question whether she felt herself sexually attracted towards women, as also to the question whether masturbation on velvet reminded her of a man. She did, however, add in amplification that she would experience a special pleasure if the velvet had touched the sexual parts of her husband. The patient displayed the sexual predilection we have described only for velvet, and not in the slightest for silks, furs or other stuffs. The choice of colour, too, has a certain significance. Most of all the patient prefers black velvet.'

Despite the fact that this case history was chosen partly to demonstrate Krafft-Ebing's basically correct belief that the attitude to intercourse was all-important in determining the fetishism of the patient, it becomes obvious that even here the dictum does not hold for women. The patient *was* a velvet fetishist, with a preference for masturbation with velvet, yet in answer to direct questions, she revealed that velvet became even more important to her when associated with the male genitals and that intercourse with her husband, if he dressed in velvet, would be even more satisfying. This undoubtedly proves our point that, for a heterosexual woman, nothing satisfactorily replaces male penetration. The woman's indifference to coitus is therefore attributable to the *absence* of velvet and not the *presence* of her husband, or any ideas about the act itself. She, like Helen K, really requires both to be fully satisfied, and her lack of enthusiasm for intercourse stems from the fact that she has found no way of introducing her fetishism into the marital act. Had she done so, it is unlikely that her case would ever have become so remarkable as to attract the attention of psychiatrists.

Some idea of what her marriage might have been can be gleaned from the relationship of Tony and Dawn B, a young couple who share a mutual sexual enthusiasm for velvet. Dawn B has been attracted by velvet since the age of about nine when she used to enjoy wrapping herself in the long velvet curtains in her parents' home. These curtains enclosed a window seat which became, during a rather lonely childhood, her 'secret place'. She could hide, cut herself off from the world by drawing the curtains and loved to stroke and feel them. Her private childhood dreams were experienced within this private caul of velvet, and her first highly satisfactory experiments with masturbation took place there. Thus from an early age Dawn B learned to associate velvet not only with pleasurable sexual sensations but also with feelings of comfort and security. These played a very important part in her first meeting with Tony. He was singing in a local amateur pop group and was dressed in tight velvet trousers and a velvet Levi jacket. This garb not only appealed to Dawn but, when he first embraced her, the feel of his velvet clothes had an erotic, as well as a very important reassuring, effect upon her. She was a timid girl and her previous sexual experiences had not been happy ones. Tony, thanks to his velvet clothes, seemed not only more desirable than other young men, but also more trustworthy and more gentle.

By some curious quirk of fate, Tony's adoption of velvet for his stage uniform was not accidental. The material was justified, of course, not only by the sartorial conventions of the pop world, but also by the group's name, was based on it. But this name, chosen by Tony, reflected a long involvement with velvet as a fetish material. Tony dates his involvement with velvet from the time he acted as a page-boy at his elder sister's wedding. For this occasion, when he would have been about twelve, he was given a pale-blue velvet suit, contact with which greatly pleased him. He liked the suit immediately because it drew a great deal of attention to him. Being the only boy and the youngest child in the family, he had always been aware, and even jealous, of the attention given to his sisters whose clothes were prettier and nicer than his. As early as eight years old he had begun to dress up in his sisters' clothes, but his velvet suit, which doting aunts and female friends claimed made him look 'very pretty', eclipsed everything else in his eyes. Furthermore, he experienced definably pleasurable sensations from the feel of the material. The velvet suit remained his most favourite possession and it was while fondling it some two years after the wedding ceremony that he became sexually excited.

'I suppose I must have had an erection before that,' Tony continued, 'but I certainly don't remember it and I'm sure I'd never consciously masturbated. But I had one that day and without thinking about it, I stripped off my jeans and pants and put on the velvet trousers. They were much too small for me, but I persevered and, at last, managed to cram myself into them. They were so tight that I couldn't possibly do them up. My penis stuck out when I sat down, it rested against the velvet. The sensation was fantastic, and just by moving my penis a very little against my velvet-covered leg, I had my first ejaculation.'

From that moment on, Tony B's attraction to velvet was fixed. Not only did the material make him feel more important, attract attention to him, but it was also associated with orgasm in his mind. Masturbation followed this discovery, of course, and always velvet was employed. As he grew older and began to take an interest in pop music, he saw in this an acceptable opportunity to indulge his passion. Having settled on the name for the group, Tony found little difficulty in persuading his mother to make his first velvet outfit, which, as he proudly claims, included velvet briefs that, unbeknown to anyone, he wore inside out.

One cannot help but remark on how well-suited Tony and Dawn B are. He needs to be the recipient of attention, she needs to take refuge in the adoration of some velvet object. She provides Tony with the attention he needs, and he represents her ideal of a partner. Fortunately, very early in their relationship, Dawn expressed her liking for Tony's velvet clothes and told him something of her childhood feelings about the material. Neither admitted immediately to their sexual involvement, but the story of Tony's velvet page-boy suit and of Dawn's private velvet place acted as a warm bond between them.

'I loved holding him, petting with him, because my hands, my face, were constantly in contact with velvet which excited me so much and made me feel so relaxed and safe. One night I told him this and he asked me to undress him. He said there would be a surprise for me. And so I did. By "surprise" I thought he meant his penis, but when I got down to his underclothes, I found that they were velvet too. He had on double-sided velvet briefs and a velvet vest.'

This act, perhaps, symbolizes their relationship. Tony occupied the role of the adored object, being undressed, receiving the maximum amount of attention and admiration while Dawn symbolically discovered that he was, as she put it, 'all velvet, right down to the skin' and thus satisfied herself that he was totally dependable and desirable. They married soon after this and their wardrobes, as well as their home, are dominated by velvet. Dawn, too, now has specially made velvet underwear and they sleep between velvet sheets. Tony also confesses that:

'Dawn made me a special double-sided velvet sheath which fits over my erect penis. We have tried it while making love and it drives her absolutely crazy. She says it's like being invaded by velvet. I like the sensation of it on my penis, but it dulls my reactions during intercourse and we don't use it very often for that reason. But I love pulling it on, and if there was some way of making it so I could rub against it while it was inside her, I'm sure I'd love it. But in order to be any good it has to fit very tightly and that way only Dawn gets any real pleasure from it. Still, I wear it for her sake because it stimulates her so much, then remove it in order to finish off.'

The awful loneliness of fetishism is completely negated in this relationship. On the contrary, their involvement with velvet is the very basis of the bond between them. It ties them closely together and creates a situation in which their fetishism can be indulged without it impinging on the rest of their lives. They are indeed fortunate.

The powerful female connotations of velvet material are remarkably demonstrated by a case of fetishism which is inextricably linked with transvestitism. In some respects Alan O's story resembles that of Tony B. So much so, in fact, that it is reasonable to suggest that had his circumstances been only slightly different, Tony B might too have been a transvestite.

'I had two sisters,' said Alan O, 'both of them older than myself. I was fiercely jealous of them. By some strange quirk of childish logic, it seemed to me that their greater popularity, as I saw it, with my father particularly, and with other relations, was directly attributable to their clothes. No one ever said how nice I looked, yet my sisters were always complimented on their pretty clothes. I had to wear grey shirts and nasty flannel shorts and I detested them. I began to "borrow" my sisters' clothes when I was about seven or eight. Mostly I got them out of the laundry basket in the bathroom. I put on everything, knickers, vests, liberty bodices, white socks, dresses and even a hair ribbon. I looked like a gorgeous little girl even then. As I got older, so I got bolder and my sisters encouraged me in dressing-up games whenever we were sure of not being disturbed. I can't remember a time when I wasn't excited by wearing girls' clothes.'

His preference for girls' clothing made of velvet was fixed in an unusual and unfortunate way. His mother had a much younger brother, a favourite uncle with all the children. Indeed, he was regarded very much as one of the children and was, in Alan O's words, 'very good looking and sexy'. Alan was fourteen when this uncle, still then only in his mid-twenties, came to live with the family. The eldest sister had already left home, and the other sister was busily leading a life of her own. The uncle, therefore, often acted as a child-minder and was alone in the house with Alan on fairly frequent occasions.

'He always left me alone, although he was very friendly towards me. I loved him, I suppose, and wanted him to take more and more notice of me. It all happened one night when my parents had gone to some function or other and he stayed in to be with me. I was up in my room and since he never came there, I took the opportunity of in-dulging in my favourite game of dressing up. I got the

125

clothes from my sister's room. A pair of frilly panties and red velvet dress. I didn't attempt, in those days, to make myself really resemble a woman. It was enough for me to wear girls' clothes. As soon as I was dressed, I was terribly excited and only the full folds of my skirt hid my thrusting erection.

'Many times when I'd dressed up in private I'd longed to show myself to someone, and that night I just couldn't resist. I must have been crazy, but I skipped out of my room and presented myself to my handsome young uncle while he sat watching television. He was startled at first, but he said I looked exactly like a little girl. I pirouetted, showing off my legs under my skirt and he asked me what else I had on. I went across to him where he lay sprawled out on a sofa and he lifted my velvet skirt. The sight of my frilly panties must have excited him for he talked about them and felt them all over. Then he asked me to sit on his knee and we pretended I was a little girl. I had a shattering orgasm inside my sister's pants, and I masturbated him.

'I felt just like a girl that night, and was convinced that my velvet dress had clinched it. It was the most becoming that I'd ever worn and that was what had attracted my uncle. After that, he tried on many occasions to play with me again, but I wouldn't let him unless I was dressed as a girl. Whenever we were alone, I'd get dressed in my sister's velvet dress and then he could do anything he liked with me.'

Today, Alan O is a confirmed transvestite. He uses female clothing to transform himself into a 'woman' and only when he is so dressed will he have sexual relations with other men. On this point he is adamant. 'How can I possibly make love to a woman? I'm not a lesbian. And I could never have sex with a man if I weren't a girl. I'm perfectly normal. I like men because there are times when I am a woman.' But because of his initial 'success' as a girl with his uncle, his female wardrobe is entirely made of velvet. Velvet underwear, velvet dresses, everything that can conceivably be made out of velvet he has acquired. Obviously, in this case the fetishist is not drawn to velvet for the intrinsic appeal (there is no suggestion, for example, that Alan O wears the plush side of the velvet next to his skin) but because of its complete association in his mind with women. As a child he recalls wanting a velvet suit because his sisters had particularly attractive velvet dresses. As far as he is concerned, velvet is the acme of femininity and therefore his 'femininity' is most strongly confirmed when he wears this material.

As we have seen, an awareness of velvet in childhood is extremely significant to later fetishistic development. In the next case, velvet is desired only marginally for itself, but primarily as a symbol of childhood and specific circumstances. Furthermore, it is velvet shorts of a very specific kind which, in fact, symbolize Ellis D's childhood and not velvet in any other form. Ellis D is now in his late thirties. A picture exists of him at the age of nine, a smiling, fair-haired boy dressed in a satin shirt and a pair of velvet shorts with cross-over braces. The shorts, as he will enthusiastically tell you, were of midnight blue silk velvet and they occupy a very important place in his life.

'My mother bought me those shorts for a special birthday party. They were expensive and I was very impressed by them. My father had died when I was very small and I had constantly been told that we couldn't afford this and that. So, having these special birthday clothes and a party was a very big treat indeed. But it stands out in my memory because of what happened subsequently. At the party, myself and another little boy stole away to show each other our penes. It was a perfectly innocent act and he instigated it. But my mother caught us and there was a terrible fuss. She sent the other boy home at once and grabbing me, put me over her knee and smacked my velvet-covered bottom.

'I hadn't, as I remember, been particularly excited by our boyish explorations, but I know my little penis grew hard the moment my mother found us. It was fright, I suppose, the exciting realization that I had been caught out in something wrong. Anyway, I had an erection sticking out of the leg of my velvet pants and I shall never, ever forget the exquisite sensation of my penis trapped and squeezed between my mother's leg and the soft, tantalizing touch of velvet when she put me across her knee. To do her justice she gave me a sound walloping, but the fiery sensation it produced in my buttocks only seemed to increase my sexual excitement. And when she had finished and I stood up, she caught hold of my penis and tucked it back inside my velvet trousers.'

The implications of this chastisement are immediately obvious. Ellis D learned to connect sexual arousal with both velvet clothing and punishment. A more dangerous combination it would be difficult to imagine. When the other small guests had gone, Ellis D's mother put him to bed, delivering a lecture on his 'disgusting' behaviour and undressing him herself. This excited him again, partly because he was afraid that he was to be beaten again, and partly through tactile stimulation. Seeing his erection, his mother again touched it and warned him that this 'nasty thing' would get him into trouble, and to underline her displeasure with her aroused son, she confiscated his party trousers.

'So from my earliest memories I've associated the pleasurable feelings of arousal with fear, punishment and velvet. I began from the time of the incident to stimulate myself, always thinking that I would be punished, or remembering my velvet trousers and the pleasant feelings I had experienced that day.'

At boarding school, Ellis D's preoccupations with velvet and punishment were given a sudden filip through another bizarre incident.

'Hemmings was a senior, a prefect and idolized by all the junior school for his sporting prowess. He was also, I see now, a sadist. Anyway, one day, when I was fifteen or so, I got into some mischief and was told to report to Hemmings' study after prayers that evening. I knew I was in for it, and that excited me very much. Sexually excited me, I mean. Well, I duly presented myself and Hemmings ticked me off and told me I would have to have six of the best. When he said that I got an erection. He told me to drop my things and to bend over the arm of a big armchair by the fireplace. Very excited, but also very afraid, I did so. I can't describe my feelings when I discovered that the chair was covered in thick brown velvet. I was even more excited and moved my penis luxuriously against the material as I waited for the strokes to fall on my bare bottom. Well, I had my six and each one seemed to increase my pleasure. It grew to a sort of frenzy. I was moaning and pushing my body against the velvet. On the last stroke, I ejaculated all over the arm of Hemmings' chair. Of course, he saw what had happened the moment I stood up and he questioned me about it. He knew what he was doing and thought it was just the beating that had aroused me, but I told him it was the velvet as well.

'I never looked back after that. Hemmings saw a willing

slave in me and used me as he liked. I became his fag immediately and we used to do all sorts of things together. He used to make me sit naked in the chair until I got all hot and excited, then he would force me to fellate him. Afterwards he would beat me for being "beastly". By the time Hemmings left the school, I was completely hooked.'

Ellis D's innate masochism which evinced itself when his mother punished him was obviously aggravated and developed by his school experiences. By the time he left school he was completely involved sexually in masochism and velvet fetishism. He is also bisexual, or as he puts it, 'It doesn't matter what sex they are, so long as they beat me.' For a time he had relations only with prostitutes, whom he paid to beat him. This, however, was unsatisfactory and he took to picking up boys who would be prepared to beat him in his own home where he was able to touch a piece of velvet. At last he realized that what he really wanted was a pair of trousers identical in every detail to those he wore at his ninth birthday party. He arranged to have these made and now wears them when he is whipped. In recent years he has become a regular advertiser in the personal contact magazines and has met several couples and individuals who are prepared to indulge his velvet fetishism and masochism. He claims that he has found many people who have an interest in velvet.

'My most satisfying experience was with a couple I met through an advertisement. I dressed in my velvet shorts and they treated me exactly like a child. The husband took me to another room where we compared our penes. I fellated him and his wife "discovered" us. She beat me with a cane on the seat of my velvet pants and I loved it.'

It is, then, in the as near as possible complete recreation of childhood and, in particular, in the first experience of punishment and sexual excitation, that the fascination of velvet lies for Ellis D. Now that he is an adult, being treated as a wayward child is doubly attractive for it increases his masochistic sensations. The childish trousers are a symbol of a childhood world which was sexually exciting because he was entirely at the mercy of others. It is in the recreation of this world that he finds his particular means of sexual fulfilment, and since he is a willing victim, he finds little difficulty in securing partners to assist in the fabrication of his childhood.

As we have seen, velvet fetishism embraces a number of other deviations, although of course it can exist quite independently. However, the case histories quoted in this chapter do go some way to showing the range of velvet fetishism which remains particularly interesting because of the unusual number of female adherents it attracts. Many velvet fetishists are, however, perfectly content to use velvet as a simple sexual substitute for the human partner. Perhaps it is the comparatively large number of female devotees which makes it a more social addiction than other forms of fetishism we have discussed. Certainly, with the exception of the transvestite case, it would be wrong to regard the majority of these people as sexually lonely. Of course, in some cases, the social aspect of their sexual lives stems from other, allied preferences, e.g. Ellis D's masochism, but it is certainly true that, for one reason or another, the velvet fetishist is less lonely and less often lonely than his peers who have some other fetishistic predilection.

In the context of this particular study, therefore, velvet fetishism is of particular interest because of the light it throws upon comparative male and female attitudes to fetishism in general and because of the range of associated deviations. In actual fact, pure velvet fetishism works in much the same way as any other form of the deviation, yet the fact remains that its devotees seem to be less isolated, less introverted, than many fetishists whose sexual proclivities isolate them instead of, as in the remarkable case of Tony and Dawn B, uniting them.

PART THREE: NATURAL FETISHISM

8: Introduction

IN some respects the whole underlying concept of fetishism can best be understood in terms of natural fetishism or partialism. As we have said, the fetish object stands in place of the human sexual partner, and many people find this easier to understand when the object is a part of the body itself which stands in place of the entire physical person. This is exactly what happens in cases of partialism, a word which is derived from the fact that the fetish object is a part of the whole, and which we call natural fetishism because the object is a portion of the natural sexual object, i.e. the human body. In many ways, too, natural fetishism clarifies the symbolism of the fetishistic ritual. The main stumbling block encountered by the layman in trying to understand the power of natural fetishism is that he instinctively assumes that the ultimate sexual expression will take the form of coitus, that is that the natural fetishist will, at the supreme moment, transfer his sexual focus from the favoured portion to the vagina. This, however, is seldom the pattern adopted by the fetishist and then only in very marginal or mild cases.

In fact, in cases of natural fetishism, Krafft-Ebing's belief that the attitude of the individual to intercourse was a determining factor in the categorization of fetishists becomes even more important. The majority of men have a special affection for some part of the female anatomy.

Most commonly it is, of course, the breasts, but we should not make the error of regarding such people as fetishists. It is by the strength of preference that the fetishist is determined; to put it another way, and to the majority of men, no matter how much they may enjoy fondling a woman's breasts, it is penetration of the vagina which most strongly attracts them and which is the desired result of all their breast-stroking and thigh-feeling. For the true partialist, this is not so. It is the breasts which attract him, and it is they which cause his orgasm. He will be disgusted by or completely indifferent to the idea of vaginal penetration. Because of the very strong possibility of confusion on this point, Krafft-Ebing's dictum must be stringently applied.

In many other areas of life we understand and accept that a part of the whole can be very revealing and can act as a microcosm or concentration of the whole's essential qualities. In art, for example, a detail of a painting, such as a photographic enlargement of a hand painted by Rembrandt, can tell us a great deal about the artist's technique and the essential elements of his style. A single metaphor can be used as an example of Keats' poetic style, or a paragraph may be lifted from a novel as being representative of the author's style and preoccupations. Natural fetishism works in much the same way. The breasts, the hands, the feet, the hair etc. can all stand as a microcosm of the female body, can exemplify the very idea of womanhood. A nude woman is the most common and universal symbol of sexuality. Her body immediately conjures up ideas of sex in the male beholder. So it is for the partial fetishist. His sexual focus has been narrowed and concentrated. Instead of seeing the whole canvas, i.e. the complete body, he receives complete sexual stimulation from one small area. And just as, after looking at, for example, a hand painted by Rembrandt in great detail, the entire canvas seems too diffuse, too large to be absorbed, so, for the natural fetishist, the whole body is insipid in comparison with the highly concentrated sexual overtones of the favoured portion. For this reason the breast fetishist will be oblivious to the whole body, will not care if the owner of fine breasts has misshapen legs and an ugly face. The essential sexuality of women will be powerfully concentrated in the breasts alone. Consequently, he will be unmoved by the sight of a woman's thighs beneath a short skirt, but deeply stirred by the cleavage of a low-cut bodice.

In the context of our previous discussions, what is most interesting in this present examination is the degree of overlapping, particularly between clothing fetishism and natural fetishism. The link between, say, glove fetishism and hand fetishism is too obvious to require comment, yet again the importance of the strength of preference must be considered. Obviously a man who is stirred by the sight of gloves cannot be ignorant of, or totally disinterested in, the hands that wear them. But we must not assume that he is one or the other without proper investigation. The two are separate, come under different categories, because of the strength of attraction. To the glove fetishist, to masturbate himself with the aid of a woman's glove will be *preferable*, more satisfying than to be masturbated by a bare-handed woman. He will be as indifferent to this act as he is to intercourse, while the natural fetishist whose attraction is to hands will regard this as the supreme, the most desirable act and will be as indifferent to gloves as he is to intercourse. Thus although we should be aware of this process of overlapping, and understand that in some cases both the part of the body and its covering play an equal part in the fetishist's addiction, we should not overstress the emphasis.

It is a question, really, of the degree of symbolism required by the fetishist, or, to put it another way, the amount of distance he needs to put between himself and the human partner. Each sort of fetishism may be regarded as a link in the chain. When the fetish object is clothing, it is the article which stands in place of the part of the body which stands in place of the partner. There are, therefore, two stages. With material fetishism, another 'layer' is added, i.e. it is the material which (frequently) stands in place of the article which stands, etc., etc. From this we can obviously conclude that natural fetishism is closest to the human partner, and accordingly that we can expect that fear of sharing sexual desire is much less strong than it is, for example, with a material fetishist. Similarly, the natural fetishist is likely to be much less involved with the physical peculiarities of the fetish object. The odour, feel and look of a part of the body is, except for the hair, virtually identical with the physical peculiarities of the body as a whole. We cannot, therefore, trace a breast fetishist's involvement to any isolated or unique qualities which significantly distinguish the breasts from the rest of the body. Skin simply does not vary that much from one part of a body to another. Nor can we look for a very complex symbolism as being the root-cause of partialism since all such symbolism will be little more than a concentration of genuine femininity.

As a result, orgasm association, or very early experiences, become even more important, and one may say even cruder in their role of determining the natural fetishist. It is not unusual to find that natural fetishism is solely determined by a redirection of the sexual focus, i.e. for the fetishist to

be fixed on the breasts, hands, etc. because of early association and for him to be virtually disinterested in the physical and symbolic connotations of the favoured part of
the body.

Once we have understood this, it becomes easier to comprehend that although the natural fetishist is in close contact with the partner, he is indifferent to normal intercourse and thus must be regarded as a true fetishist. He sees
the favoured part of the body, for a variety of reasons, as
complete in itself and therefore does not wish to express
himself via coitus. For example, if it is the hands of a
woman that attract him, he will regard them as the sexual
organ and will wish to be masturbated by the woman.
He is at once more social than other fetishists, simply because he cannot make contact with a part of the body without the presence of the whole, and more keenly anti-social
in that he is oblivious to or ignores the greater part of the
whole. And since the partner inevitably has sexual needs
of her own, she is doomed to frustration by the fetishist's
concentration on her breasts, feet or whatever. As a result,
it is extremely difficult for the natural fetishist to find willing partners. He invariably has recourse to some unsatisfactory, anti-social behaviour, e.g. assault, to prostitutes or
to pornography. It is, too, the most acutely denigrating
form of fetishism. Psychologically it is much worse for a
woman to be 'reduced' to a pair of breasts, or a hank of
hair, than to be symbolized by a pair of pants. She can be
ignorant of the latter, but must play a particularly de-
meaning passive role in the former. She cannot escape her
denigration which is, of course, a big factor in the enforced
loneliness of the natural fetishist.

Finally we should note that, unlike velvet fetishism, partialism seldom attracts women. It is an approach to sexual-

ity which is fundamentally alien to feminine psychology. Their instinct is to build up the partner, and not to reduce him. They are dependent for complete satisfaction on their temporary, ritualistic subjection by the male, and it is difficult to envisage or express this when only a fraction of the whole is enjoyed and desired. A woman requires a complete man, and at the moment of intercourse her abandonment is to him entirely. She cannot accept a portion as a symbolic substitute without becoming frustrated. Like so many other branches of fetishism, then, this is very much a male preserve, which depends entirely on the reduction of the woman to a small, passive, part.

We have also included an aspect of fetishism which is loosely, but significantly, connected to natural fetishism. This is defect or injury fetishism, a rare manifestation of our subject which is, however, of considerable interest. In such cases, the fetish object is some deformity, such as a hunched back, or some injury such as a bandaged wound. The fetishist, however, does not seek sexual contact with the deformity, but this is the source of his or her attraction to the partner. The attitude to intercourse is not so important in these cases, indeed it is frequently the means of consummation. However, the defect fetishist will have no interest in a partner who is whole and healthy. This is a very emotional, deeply psychological form of the aberration which obeys a rather different set of laws. However, it throws light on the whole problem of fetishism and should perhaps best be regarded as a corollary to our other discussions.

9: Parts of the Body

THE one part of the body which, when regarded as a fetish object, exerts the sort of complex and various attraction which we expect of a fetish object is hair. The hair has definite physical attributes which appeal to the fetishist, and which can be discovered and valued much as a piece of clothing or material is. Its tactile, visual and odoriferous qualities all play a part in the fetishist's addiction. For example, it has been held by certain experts that a woman's hair holds a specific concentration of the so-called *odor di femina* and that thus, for some men, the scent of the hair, which it should not be forgotten is made up of a series of elongated scent organs, is particularly stimulating.* Furthermore, we are all familiar with the adage 'a woman's hair is her crowning glory'. This popular phrase is indicative of a symbolism associated with the hair that has recently lost much of its force. Long hair has for years been associated with women. Women grew their hair as long as possible, took elaborate care of it, and dressed it, to complete their decorative appearance. Thus hair became an accepted symbol of femininity which has, in recent years, become confused and altered as more and more women have followed the fashion for short, easily managed hair and a similar number of men have grown theirs longer and longer and taken better care of it. It has been suggested that many men have grown their hair because it increases their attractiveness for the opposite sex. This may well be true,

* See *The Sweet Smell of Sex* by Richard K. Champion, Canova Press, London, 1969.

although unproven. It seems, at least in the light of present information, that long hair in men is more directly attributable to social protest and as a logical extension of the masculine adoption of a decorative image. Hair, in fact, has a dual symbolism. Long hair remains primarily a feminine symbol, while body hair, which is, of course, much more common in men, is regarded as a sign of manliness. This latter point is certainly not without its attraction to some women and can often be seen in the feminine fondness for beards and moustaches on men.

In short, hair fetishism may be regarded as a bridge between the common forms of fetishism as discussed in this book and the specialized attractions of parts of the body proper. These differences and similarities can best be demonstrated by the study of a specific case.

Even as a small child Nigel N showed a remarkable fondness for his girl companions and sisters. He was gentle and considerate, winning praise and commendation from his parents and their friends for his lack of boyish roughness and aggression. He used to brush his younger sister's hair and loved to stroke the long locks of any little girl who would allow him this intimacy. As a result he was considered 'a nice, gentle little boy'.

'What nobody realized,' said Nigel, 'is that stroking a girl's hair made me feel very sexy, even then. I liked the feel of it, of its softness and strength. I loved the silky sheen of well-cared-for hair, its waves and curls and ringlets. I liked the way it framed the face, and to me it always smelt sweet and feminine. By the age of about ten, I can recall having erections when I stroked and smelt a girl's long hair. I used to do it so much because it excited me, made me feel so many lovely sensations.'

We see at once from this statement that Nigel N could

be talking about any of the fetish objects we have already discussed. His response was entirely physical. His hands responded to the texture of hair, his imagination was fired by its smell and his eye delighted in its appearance. It was, in all these particulars, a true fetish object. And until the age of thirteen, his was a quite natural fondness. He simply liked hair and his awareness of its sexual implications were, at the time, quite unconscious.

'When I was thirteen I spent two weeks in the country with my aunt. She only had one child, a beautiful girl called Belinda, my cousin, whose long, slightly waving and very thick blonde hair reached down below her shoulder blades. I was completely captivated by her hair from the very moment I saw her. Belinda was about eighteen months older than me and much more sexually precocious. She used to let me stroke her hair and even bury my face in it while she discussed with me the few scraps of sexual knowledge we had. We went through the childish ritual of comparing our privates, showing ourselves to each other. This interested her far more than me. The sight of her vagina meant nothing to me, but she had an endless curiosity about my penis. So we used to spend hours together with me stroking her hair and smelling it while she explored and examined my erect penis. I became immensely excited, and one day, while we were doing this, I knew that something unusual, something new was happening. I didn't know what, but in fact it was the approach of my first orgasm. We were, in fact, lying down. I had her hair spread out like a golden, perfumed curtain across my face, while she was touching my penis, squeezing it slightly in her hand. As the delicious tension mounted in me, I suddenly thought how marvellous it would be to place my penis among the thick waves of her lustrous hair. I knelt up.

Belinda offered no resistance, being as innocent as me about male ejaculation. I pressed my throbbing organ against the side of her head and twined locks of her hair about it. It was marvellous and in a second I had my first orgasm. We were both amazed by the phenomenon, and Belinda was, not unnaturally, very angry at having my ejaculation in her hair. She never allowed me to do it again. I had to content myself for the rest of our time together with touching her hair while she played with my penis, but it wasn't nearly as exciting as having my penis itself in contact with her hair.'

Here we see the normal pattern of orgasm association which fixes the fetish as a necessary requirement of sexual release. This is generally, as we have said, even more crucial in cases of partialism, although in this particular case, the other, more usual fetish requirements are also fulfilled.

After his encounter with Belinda, Nigel N became totally absorbed by hair. He never dared to repeat the pleasurable experiment he had enjoyed with his cousin, but he still sought contact with women's hair and frequently experienced involuntary ejaculations as a result. He also began to collect hairs from his sister's hairbrush and bound these around his penis during masturbation. However, this did not satisfy him, for he longed to have thick swathes of hair with which to cover and bind his penis. He was, of course, exclusively attracted to girls with long, thick hair and all his girl-friends during his teens possessed beautiful hair which he was able to caress and smell. He generally achieved orgasm during this contact.

'When I was about twenty, I went out with a girl with very long chestnut-coloured hair which I liked enormously. One day she announced her intention of having it all cut off. At first I was dismayed and tried to dissuade her, and then I realized what an opportunity this was for me. I agreed, but insisted that she let me have the tresses that were cut off. She thought, of course, that this was a very romantic and charming wish of mine and readily agreed. The moment I saw her with short, cropped hair I lost interest in her, but she handed me a box with her hair in it and I was thrilled to the very marrow of my bones. I couldn't wait to get home, to strip off and lay my hands on the hair. With trembling hands and throbbing penis I opened the box and picked out a thick swathe of her hair. It still smelt of her and felt like a hank of living silk. I sat on the edge of my bed quivering with desire, and without thought just began to lash at my stiff, upstanding penis with the hair. It was the most exquisite sensation I'd ever experienced, and after a few strokes I had a magnificent orgasm.'

Once again the masturbatory use to which Nigel N put his girl-friend's hair parallels that of any other inanimate fetish object but, of course, this is a peculiar attribute of hair which cannot be accomplished with other parts of the body because it is not possible to divorce them in this harmless way from the person as a whole. However, Nigel N had got what he wanted, what he had always wanted, and this plus his girl-friend's short hair made him lose all interest in her. He devoted himself entirely to masturbation with the hair she had given him.

'I tied it securely into three thick swathes. With them I would "whip" my penis, fold them around my erection, bury it in them and titillate my buttocks, perineum and testicles until I reached orgasm.'

But hair, once it has been cut, soon dies. It loses its odour and lustre and before long Nigel N had to seek new ways of being in contact with female hair. His frustration grew for now nothing satisfied him unless he bring his penis into contact with female hair. And, of course, none of his succession of long-haired girl-friends would satisfy him in this way. In desperation he began to visit prostitutes who were prepared to meet his specific requirements. As a result, he ceased to have girl-friends at all and, at last, entered into a semi-permanent paid relationship with a prostitute which lasted for some time.

'She had beautiful long blonde hair and I used to knot locks of it around my penis and let her lead me about like that. She never objected to my ejaculating in her hair, and I suppose she made me happier than any woman I have ever known besides Belinda.'

He has also been able to come to an arrangement with a hairdresser who sells him female hair at intervals. This and his occasional visits to prostitutes make up the sum of his sexual life. He has never had intercourse and rejects the idea that he ever could. He dislikes pubic hair, condemning it as 'nasty, coarse stuff'. He likes to look at photographs of long-haired women and to read descriptions of female hair. He frequently masturbates over such photographs and articles. The very sound and sight of the word is exciting to him, and he has been known to follow girls with long hair in the street. Only by great resistance is he able to prevent himself touching the long hair of women in the street and on public transport. Male hair, wigs and hair-pieces do not interest him at all. Of course, his curious predilection has cut him off from women and he knows that he cannot marry, for he has no wish to have any sexual contact with women except for their hair.

In its loneliness and limitations, Nigel N's case is a good example of the general effects of partialism. We see how the human partner is reduced and how difficult it is for him to obtain the special contact he desires. Yet he is more fortunate in one way than the breast and buttock fetishists, for example, because it is possible for him to obtain the desired part without directly involving himself with a woman.

A very unusual case which reveals another aspect of hair fetishism was recounted by London and Caprio.* The patient concerned, although married, regularly masturbated while indulging in bizarre fantasies.

'I try not to touch my penis when I masturbate. I lie on my stomach and indulge in fantasies. The images I conjure up are women (pick-ups off the street corner). Sometimes it involves a girl of my acquaintance, perhaps a sister of one of my associates, to whom I have scarcely spoken in real life. Just how the conflict of images is initiated I cannot say – perhaps it occurs in comparing the physical attributes of one girl with those of another – I am not sure. This I do know – in order to qualify as an image for my fantasy the girl involved has to have ravishing hair. I can remember in real life I was overcome and awe-stricken by the "beauty" of any girl with a mass of lustrous hair, regardless of colour, as long as it had a beautiful sheen. Actually the girls involved are far from beautiful. Also, virtually all the girls involved are forward and of an aggressive nature, hence in my fantasy each seems to be trying to outdo the other, the idea seeming to be that each is endeavouring to show the other that she is a "better woman" by the fury or deep-seatedness of her carnal manifestations. In later life I found myself consciously making "matches" for the women I met in real life. I would match one against

* L. S. London & F. S. Caprio, *Sexual Deviations*, Linacre Press, Washington, 1950.

another of equal bodily proportions and length and thickness of hair. Most often these people did not know each other in real life. More recently the conflict has narrowed itself to some extent to one between a woman with over a yard of jet black hair and the other with the same amount of red hair.'

Later in the investigations into this case, the patient revealed a more specific fantasy. For example :

'The two women approach each other. They either rub each other's hair or pull it. Then they embrace in an aggressive way. Each of them is nude and they display their charms in the sense of competition. They contact their bodies, rubbing each other's sex parts.

'These two women have an utter contempt for each other. They've been girls of high moral character, haughty girls whom you would scarcely conceive of indulging in such combat. They're of heavy build. I'm able to achieve an ejaculation each time when I have a fantasy of this kind – even more so than sexual intercourse. More recently the women are in contest. The woman defeated would be lying down, writhing in humiliation. The other woman would contemptuously walk away. It's the intermingling of the hair and the contempt which they show in their eyes that is most erotic.'

There are, obviously, strong overtones of sado-masochism in these fantasies of hair-pulling and further investigation suggested that the patient identified most strongly with the defeated woman. The root of his peculiar form of hair fetishism was later traced, as we would expect, to a childhood incident involving the patient's sister.

'I was perhaps twelve years old at the time – my sister was in her room at home (she was perhaps fifteen) and I was in mine. As was often the case, we were bantering back

146

and forth, calling each other names etc. when we suddenly decided on a test of strength.

'I remember we went in on her bed and proceeded to wrestle with each other (fully clothed). My sister had at that time a mass of long, black, dark hair that hung to her shoulders. I remember that I was nearly smothered by the thickness of her thatch. I was getting the worst of it most of the time and she was on top of me, pinning me down. However, I didn't mind the smothering, but held her even closer, enjoying ecstatic sensations as our bodies writhed together. I actually had an ejaculation before we broke apart, upon the approach of our mother, who did not suspect that it was anything other than an ordinary fight.'

From this it becomes obvious that the patient's fantasies are a means of re-creating this pleasurable incident from childhood. In the fantasy he identifies with the defeated woman, the idea of humiliation associated with contact with hair being the element that excites him to orgasm. The case is particularly interesting because it indicates an abstraction of a common element in hair fetishism which is peculiar to the aberration and which has very strong elements of sado-masochism. An illustration is provided by the case of George W who was arrested and charged with common assault after snipping off a lock of hair from a girl's head. It will be obvious from our introductory remarks that this particular sort of behaviour is greatly influenced by the need to obtain contact at all costs with beautiful hair. In desperation, the fetishist who has no permissible outlet for his particular needs cannot resist the temptation to 'steal' a lock of hair by forcibly cutting it from the scalp of an admired woman.

But there is more to this process than the desperate need to obtain the fetish object, as further investigation of

George W's case revealed. His sexual contact with women had always been via hair and there had been very few of these during his lifetime. His fetishism was rooted in a childhood jealousy of his mother's and sister's long and beautiful hair. He, too, had wanted to grow shoulder-length hair which was, as far as he was concerned, the very height of beauty and attractiveness. Naturally enough, his parents had forbidden any such thing, and his sexual involvement with female hair was consequently mixed with jealousy, which manifested itself in a wish to destroy that which he could not have. Hair was denied him on two counts. Firstly he could not grow his own, and secondly he was forbidden sexual contact with female hair. Thus he had a sadistic desire to revenge himself on women for this denial. When he produced his scissors and cut a lock of hair from an innocent girl, he was symbolically destroying that which was forbidden to him. He had, in fact, no use for the hair, for although his sole sexual outlet was masturbation, he did not indulge himself in this way with the aid of hair. In fact, he had an orgasm at the moment of cutting the lock and threw it away the moment he had obtained it. His solitary masturbation was accompanied by fantasies of girls with long, lustrous hair which he destroyed or polluted by ejaculation. In this particular again we see that hair fetishism has close affinities with clothing fetishism which further emphasizes that it is a bridge between general fetishism and partialism. Just as a man sometimes desires to pollute and spoil a pair of panties as a symbol of women, so also the instinct to destroy the hair can play its part in hair fetishism.

We have already briefly referred to the female response to male hair, and have indicated that very few women really qualify as hair fetishists. Yet we should not forget that body hair is an accepted symbol of masculinity and that copious chest hair, for example, often increases a man's attractiveness for some women. This is, however, simply a sign to the woman that her partner is completely and thoroughly masculine. She does not seek to replace him by his body hair. Similarly, many men are attracted by women with hair-covered legs and unshaven armpits. However, this is merely a part of the woman's general attraction and the presence of this so-called 'superfluous' hair does not act as a true fetish object. On the question of long hair in men, there is little reliable evidence. It is certainly probable that this greater length of hair increases and intensifies the general masculine smell, which certainly appeals to many women, but there is no indication as yet that women are becoming sexually involved with the flowing locks adopted by so many young men at the present moment.

The nearest one can come to discovering a genuine female sexual awareness of male hair is via beards and moustaches. Even so, this is not true hair fetishism, but certainly for women like Jean it increases a man's sexual attraction.

'I've always preferred hairy men,' she said, 'largely because all the men in my family have a lot of body hair. I mean that, as an adolescent girl, my first awareness of the difference between the sexes was the respective prevalence and absence of body hair. The fact that my brother had a penis and I a vagina meant little to me. What impressed me was that he and my father both had thick, curly chest hair and very hirsute legs whereas I, and all the women I knew, had none at all. I suppose you would say that I am very hair-conscious, and to me there is something repugnant about a man who has a hairless body.

149

'For this reason I've always tried to choose hirsute men, and I have a definite preference for beards and moustaches. There is another reason for this, though. I am addicted to oral sex, and a beard really adds something to cunnilingus. My present man friend has a big bushy beard and I encourage him to rub it against my vagina quite roughly before and during oral sex. It stimulates me a great deal, but apart from that one act, I just prefer hairy men to smooth ones.'

Jean L is correct to regard herself as someone who is hair-conscious rather than a hair fetishist. She prefers hirsute men simply because her earliest awareness of the opposite sex taught her to expect them to be hairy. It is a simple masculine symbol, and as a result of this favouring of body hair, she has discovered the extra stimulus provided by beards during cunnilingus. By no interpretation of the facts of this case can she be regarded as a hair fetishist.

As we have said, the single biggest difference between hair fetishism and other forms of natural fetishism is that it is possible, although admittedly difficult, for the devotee to obtain contact with his desired fetish object without actually being in the presence of a partner. Hair can be cut off, it can be obtained from hairdressers, but other parts of the body can only be enjoyed fetishistically with the aid and participation of the partner, and since very few women are willing to be reduced in this way to some localized area of their anatomy, such fetishists generally experience great difficulty in establishing contact with the desired object.

By far the most common form of natural fetishism is that which fixes the sexual focus on the female breasts. No other part of a woman's body is so easily seen and so obviously symbolic of femininity. The breasts have associations for men from their very earliest moments of life. Food and comfort are provided by the mother's breasts and later in life they become obvious erotic objects. The breasts are, in fact, a male child's first awareness of another sex. They embody the very idea of womanhood and no matter how subconscious that awareness may be, few men are immune to their symbolism. Man begins his life in intimate contact with them and in early adolescence learns to regard them as sexual objects. Women's clothes invariably stress the breasts and they are the most obvious symbol of the anatomical differences between male and female. Furthermore the breasts are highly erogenous to most women who will permit a man contact with them when other intimacies are denied. Bearing this in mind, it would seem comparatively easy for a breast fetishist to obtain the contact he desires, but this is not often so if he is a true fetishist, like Ted F.

'The only thing that interests me about a woman is her breasts. I don't care how old or ugly a woman may be, as long as she has big firm breasts. I have no interest in anything else. During my life I have twice tried to have intercourse with a woman but neither time could I get an erection. I only tried because it was expected of me, and I've never wanted to make love to a woman in that way.

'I was breast-fed as a baby and frequently saw my mother's breasts as a child. I am the eldest of five children and I can remember being terribly jealous when I saw my mother breast-feeding my brothers and sisters. Jealous and excited. I could watch for hours, but I always had the desire to push the baby away and suck my mother's nipple myself.

'Yes, I used to spy on my mother as I got older and loved to see her breasts. I was fourteen when my youngest

151

brother was born, and I had an erection when I first saw him feeding. After that I used to sit by my mother at feeding times whenever I could and would masturbate through the pocket of my trousers as I watched. I always had an orgasm. My masturbatory fantasies were always to do with breasts, with being able to suck and handle them.

'When I first started going out with girls it was only their breasts that interested me. I wasn't even interested in kissing. I just wanted the maximum contact with their breasts. I quickly discovered that I had a very weak response to contact with breasts covered in clothing. I actively disliked the feel of a brassiere and would immediately try to get at the naked breasts. I never went with a girl more than once if she wouldn't let me handle her naked breasts.

'Once I'd uncovered the breasts, I would squeeze and caress them, play with the nipples and suck them. I always had an orgasm while doing this without even touching myself. Unfortunately, I soon learned that girls who would let me do what I wanted with their breasts were generally ones for whom breast manipulation was extremely stimulating. This meant that they usually wanted intercourse as a result of this arousal. As I said, I tried on two occasions, when I hadn't ejaculated, but with hopeless results. Normally there was no point in even trying because I had already had an ejaculation. After this had happened a few times, none of my girl-friends wanted to go on seeing me and it became increasingly difficult to find a girl who would let me just feel her breasts.

'I began to masturbate more and more and about this time I started to get a very strong erotic feeling in my own nipples. From that I used to imagine that I had breasts of my own. While I masturbated, I could imagine having big breasts sprouting from my own chest and I would fan-

152

tasize that by bending down I could bring my penis into contact with these phantom breasts. Because of this fantasy, I longed to touch my penis with a woman's breasts.

'At last I realized that the only hope of getting what I wanted was to go to a prostitute. I was terribly nervous, especially as I knew they would think I wanted to have intercourse. But I plucked up courage and explained to a big-breasted girl who agreed to do what I wanted. That was marvellous. I could do whatever I liked and after all the usual breast play, I placed my throbbing organ between her big, warm breasts and pressed them on to it until I ejaculated.

'That is what I like doing best and, when I can afford it, I go to a prostitute and indulge myself in that way. I always choose ones with big breasts and they seldom object to my requests. I still go out with girls when I can, but it never lasts very long because they soon get tired of the fact that I am only interested in their breasts. There's nothing in it for them, you see, and I can understand how they feel. Mostly now I masturbate with the aid of fantasies, and sometimes of photographs. I have a lot of pictures of women's breasts, but only a few meet my requirements. I like everything else to be covered, like the impression that her breasts are hanging out of her clothes, preferably with the model leaning forward so that they swing outwards. Strip shows and nude films excite me visually, but after a while it gets frustrating not being able to handle the breasts on display.'

Ted F is completely breast orientated and has a sound grasp of his situation. The woman as a whole is generally anonymous as far as he is concerned. Only the breasts and complete, intimate contact with them is of interest to him. There is, as we see from his statement, no aversion to intercourse, to the natural object of sexual desire. His fetishism is simply the result of a total focusing of attention on the breasts. His need is partly linked with his desire for a mother, and we should not by any means discount the jealousy he felt on seeing his brothers and sisters at his mother's breasts. Emotionally, he is trying to reassert his claim on his mother. Sexually, the breasts stand in place of the entire woman. Being the eldest child, he obviously felt that his mother was exclusively his and felt rejected when the other babies were given access to her breasts. It is in compensation for this that he seeks the breasts of other women. The anonymity of the prostitute suits his purposes well, but his circumstances do not permit him to indulge very often in this way. Consequently for much of his life he suffers from sexual frustration and his normal relationships with women are completely impaired by his special sexual and emotional requirements.

The case of David N is at once more peripheral, more specialized and more obviously disturbing. David N is a married man whose domestic life was reasonably happy, despite the fact that his sexual relations with his wife were only ever intermittent and generally unsatisfactory. There are no children. He explains:

'I had never had sexual relations with a woman before I married. We had petted quite heavily, but I was the male equivalent of a virgin on my wedding night. It had never occurred to me that I wouldn't like intercourse. I had always been aroused by our sexual games before marriage and just assumed that intercourse would be the logical and most satisfying end to our sexual relationship. What affected me was the sight of my wife's buttocks. They were large and soft and I took an instant dislike to them. I could not consummate the marriage for several nights, and when

I did manage it, it was by thinking the whole time about nice, neat, tight, muscular buttocks.'

David N's wife does not appear to be a very highly sexed woman, and their marriage has survived the sexual difficulties he unwittingly brought to it. The idea of firm, small buttocks persisted in his mind and grew into a series of fantasies which enabled him to have sexual relations with his wife. As a result of this preoccupation, David N began to take more and more notice of buttocks, to observe and compare them. This led to a conclusion which profoundly shocked him.

'I suddenly realized that it was male buttocks that attracted me. I never saw a woman that had that high, tight muscularity of the buttocks which attracted me and which characterizes the buttocks of young men and boys. I had never had any homosexual tendencies before this time and the idea of having sexual relations with one of my own sex disgusted me. It still does. Yet the only thing that attracted me was beautiful male buttocks. I would get an erection just seeing them in the street, and I had to stop going to the swimming baths because my reactions were too embarrassing. I tried very hard to resist this awful attraction, but I simply couldn't. In the street, on the underground, everywhere I found myself looking at male buttocks. The whole thing became too much for me when I was travelling on a very crowded tube train one evening and suddenly found myself forced up against the buttocks of a young man. Even through our combined clothing I could feel their shape and firmness and I ejaculated simply as a result of this contact.'

It is not surprising that David N should be haunted by the spectre of his own homosexuality and there is no doubt that he struggled against this sudden, overwhelming desire for contact with the male buttocks. He fantasized, however, more and more on the subject and only with the aid of these fantasies was he able to conduct any sexual relationship with his wife. But already he found that he preferred solitary masturbation to intercourse because he felt less guilty about indulging in his fantasies.

'Things went from bad to worse and one evening I just couldn't face it any longer. I went straight from the office to a pub. I began a steady evening's drinking, and by closing time I was pretty drunk. I started to wend my way home but I got picked up by a young man. I mean that I had been staring at his buttocks as he walked along the street, as I always did, and suddenly he was talking to me. He said that if I'd got five pounds I could go home with him. I agreed. He took me to a room somewhere. I don't remember where. I was both excited and afraid. I didn't know what to do. I knew I ought to go home and yet I couldn't take my eyes off his bottom.

'He undressed, stripped completely and came to me. My eyes focused on his body, his penis with disgust. I pushed him round and the sight of his buttocks excited me wildly. I held him still and caressed his bottom, kissed it. Fumbling, I got out my penis and laid it against the firm cheeks. He was annoyed at that. He said, very crudely, that he didn't go for anal intercourse. It had never occurred to me. It took me a moment to realize what he meant. Of course he thought that I was trying to, well, have anal intercourse with him. As soon as I realized that, I lost my erection. I suppose I suddenly realized what a terrible level I had sunk to. I began to lash out at his bottom. I lost all control of my senses for a moment, and then he put a leather belt in my hand and I was whipping his buttocks. It excited and disgusted me at the same time. I ejaculated over him,

156

eventually, and feeling sick and full of self-disgust, I got a cab home.'

Despite his very violent reactions to this bizarre encounter, David N has repeated it on two occasions, and since that first time, he has not had intercourse with his wife. This is a very complex and in some ways very baffling case. No amount of questioning and probing revealed any childhood incident or homosexual contact which could explain his sudden desire for buttocks of a particular shape and kind. It can only be concluded that his fairly comprehensive ignorance of female anatomy and the sex act had led him to confuse the buttocks in some way with the vagina. It is conceivable that he thought, through some now forgotten misinformation of his childhood, that copulation was effected *per anus*. If this is so, then he would be familiar with the male buttocks and would, given his ignorance, possibly expect that part of the female anatomy to be exactly similar. He married a large, fleshy-buttocked woman who by no means represented his ideal. By looking around for a physical counterpart of the perfect, shapely buttocks which he imagined, the realization that only male buttocks met his requirements was forcibly brought home to him. Discovering this desired object only increased his innate dislike of intercourse.

Despite his extraordinary predilection and bizarre behaviour, it seems certain that David N, despite his fears, is neither a homosexual nor a flagellant. He is, certainly, a buttock fetishist and, as we know, it is common for fetishists to desire only one type of the object they favour. Thus it is necessary to understand that it is not the *maleness* of the buttocks that attracts him but their shape and muscularity, a specific shape which is only commonly found in men. This absence of a homosexual impulse is confirmed by the fact that he has an aversion to any other part of the male body and that the idea of committing anal intercourse is completely repulsive to him. He has no oral or tactile contact with men, other than with the buttocks and even then he complains that the inevitable sight of muscular, hairy legs annoys him.

It is because he fears that his fetishism invokes a homosexual impulse that he likes to beat, smack and whip the buttocks. He is in fact symbolically punishing the male partner for the imputation of his own homosexuality. He is attempting to destroy the fetish object which exerts such a powerful and unwanted hold over him. Because of the masculinity of the owners of the desired fetish object, he punishes it and himself. As a result of this complex and distressing focus, David N is made very miserable and his marriage is fundamentally threatened. Very little can be done to help him without some key to the cause of this strange aberration. However, it has been possible to alleviate his fears of incipient homosexuality and every effort is being made to discover some clue, some explanation of this fixation, which should, once explained in simple terms, help him to free himself from the grip of a peculiarly destructive form of buttock fetishism.

Finally, let us look at examples of foot fetishism. Krafft-Ebing recorded a case in which the patient adored the sweaty, swollen feet of factory and manual workers and who obtained orgasm simply by imagining that he had such ugly and ill-treated feet. In this case, a peculiar form of masochism was undoubtedly at work. Other men have worshipped the delicate feet of women, often for a variety of masochistic and emotive reasons discussed earlier under the heading of boot fetishism. A reasonably straightforward case of true foot fetishism is provided by Bill M who is entranced by naked female feet so long as they be clean and well shaped. On the beach, it is the naked feet of women and not their partially exposed bodies which excite him. He likes to caress, kiss and hold the naked feet of a woman. In this he indulges in an act of worship, of self-denigration, but he does not seek to experience pain or any more overt form of masochism. Shoes do not interest him at all, except in his masturbatory fantasies.

'I like to imagine that I am a shoe, filled by a beautiful foot. I can imagine the toes touching me, being squeezed by the tight leather, the contact of instep and heel. It is ecstasy to imagine myself transformed into a soft leather shoe which is in complete and total contact with a nice foot.'

Having kissed and caressed the foot, he presses it to his groin and likes to move his penis against the sole and to have his erection teased, pressed and caressed by both feet which quickly brings him to orgasm. This is usually accomplished with the aid of prostitutes, but during the hippie boom, when bare feet were common, he persuaded several girls to indulge him in this way for a small sum of money.

As an adolescent he recalls a picnic one hot summer day. He was dressed in a pair of shorts and fell asleep. His sister woke him and teased him by tickling his legs and groin with her bare foot. He remembers waking and allowing her to excite and arouse him in this way while he was able to stare up her skirt to her underwear. At the crucial moment he seized her foot and pressed it on to his penis, ejaculating immediately. His predilection in fact results from a simple case of orgasm association. In subsequent years he has sought to reproduce this situation in so far as he likes his partners to be clothed and to be able to look up their skirts while he makes contact with the feet. He does not touch any other part of the body, and has not had intercourse, nor does he wish to do so.

We have looked now at some of the major parts of the body which commonly become the sole concern of the sexual focus and thus fetish objects. But, of course, any area of the body – the thighs, the hands, the ears, the armpits – can also serve in this way. We have chosen the more common parts because they are representative of the whole range of natural fetishism and because by choosing extreme and bizarre examples, it is possible to show that natural fetishism is by no means as straightforward as its inevitable association with the normal sex-object would, at first, lead us to suppose. It is, in some ways, the most comprehensible and the most extreme form of fetishism. Simply because of its close link with the human partner it tends to dramatize the whole concept of fetishism in a way which makes the aberration perhaps easier to understand than when one is dealing with what are, in essence, abstract symbols.

10: Physical Defects and Injuries

A CURIOUS off-shoot of natural fetishism is that which is concerned with bodily defects. Once again a part of the body acts as the fetish object but with this difference, that it must be in some way defective or injured. Thus, to give an example, it may be the foot which attracts the fetishist, but in this category the foot must be misshapen, e.g. a club foot, and generally such a festishist will not be interested in the normal, properly functional foot. Even superficial injuries can exert this peculiar form of attraction and in such cases the sight of a bandage, or a piece of sticking plaster, will sexually attract the susceptible.

For most people any sort of bodily defect or injury is more likely to occasion a feeling of revulsion or distanced compassion, and so strong are these feelings that defect fetishism at first fills people with horror and often remains incomprehensible. It consequently becomes more important than ever that we understand the psychological motives behind this attraction and in this particular form of fetishism it is primarily the feelings of the fetishist which provide the clue to his particular interest. The physical qualities of the defect or injury are only peripherally important and overt sexual contact with the defective or injured part is comparatively rare. If this seems to suggest that defect fetishism is a relatively simple form of the aberration, it should be made quite clear at once that the emotional reasons for such attractions are very complex indeed. This fact is complicated by (a) the rareness of the condition and (b) the fact that since it seldom results in any anti-social behaviour or direct sexual contact, the researcher has very few opportunities of discovering more about it.

The first clues which we can use to give us a more general insight into this strange sexual desire are provided by the reactions to defects and injuries of the normal human being. As we have said, these are generally ones of horror or compassion, or perhaps more accurately a mixture of both emotions. Two basic human instincts are involved here. We feel horror at the sight of a club foot or a bandaged head because we interpret this evidence of defectiveness as a threat to us. We have a sensation of another's pain, of the unpleasantness of being physically limited in some way. We think, 'There, but for the grace of God, go I' and we have an irrational fear that contact in any way with such an injured person will somehow taint or threaten us. But, as we know if we have any comprehension at all of the masochistic impulse, the most commonly frightening things can be sexually stirring to some people. So it is that one cause of defect fetishism is a masochistic feeling of worship of the injured, the defective. Such people feel that they are in close contact with pain and damage, concepts which they find thrilling. To them the club foot or withered arm is a symbol of some universal sadism, some cruelty, perhaps attributable to God or Nature, which makes life, in their view, more attractive because more dangerous. A wound or injury reminds them that sadists exist, that some men beat their wives, for example, and they take a vicarious sexual pleasure in identifying with the injured person who is more 'fortunate' than they. For this reason such people will never willingly accept that a black eye, for example, has been caused by some natural accident. To them it is always the mark of some sadistic bully who has wantonly caused pain and injury which they are able to 'share' through association with the injured person.

Compassion for the injured, the defective, is equally strong and also motivates some defect fetishists. This is again a basic human instinct and a laudable one. It stems from the gregarious impulse to protect, a parallel of sorts with the animals' instincts to protect the young and the weak until they are able to play their proper part in the life of the herd. A person with a physical defect is vulnerable, as is one who temporarily incapacitated by some injury. In some people there is a strong impulse to help and protect such a person and this, too, can be exaggerated until it becomes a form of fetishism. Slowly, only the helpless appear attractive, and the fetishist gains a sense of power, perceived sexually, over the injured person. This is not, however, necessarily a destructive power. It is not always an example of the fundamentally timid person who draws strength from another's greater vulnerability. Frequently it is akin to that compassion which makes saints. The sense of being needed, of being able to share their own necessarily greater strength, provides a kind of sexual ecstasy. This is an emotion which is also akin to the maternal instinct and, as a result, women are frequently drawn to disabled men in a subconsciously fetishistic way. Such women must, of course, be distinguished from those who care for the injured and defective out of a selfless love, which is also an admirable attribute of the female sex. Others, however, deliberately seek the halt and the lame partly to indulge a powerful or frustrated maternal instinct which is, obviously, closely allied to their sexual impulses. On occasions the two become so strongly confused that the women concerned can be regarded as defect fetishists.

The principles of contrast and identification are strongly at work here. A defect fetishist either finds strength, a sexually experienced sense of self-aggrandizement through association with the less fortunate, or is sexually aroused masochistically by identification with the injured and infirm. In either case the contrast is indicative of some personal weakness on the part of the fetishist. It usually means that he or she lacks something in themselves, that they feel inferior and only by false comparison, i.e. comparison with the unnaturally diminished, do they feel complete and important.

There are, too, cases of defect fetishism which are directly attributable to orgasm association. By some chance, sexual arousal has early been associated with some physical disability and subsequently the individual seeks out defectives or the injured in an attempt to recapture the early circumstances. Curiously, this early association may be connected with some injury of their own, which is later re-experienced via some other person. We shall study examples of this aspect of the fetishism in due course.

There is, finally, also the sadistic motivation, although this is fortunately rare. In such cases, the fetishist harbours sadistic impulses which are, in a sense, fulfilled by association with defective or injured persons. Usually this indicates a *latent* form of sadism which is sufficiently gratified by an awareness of the injury. Very occasionally, the constant presence of that injury incites the sadist to inflict others. Many such people find satisfaction in knowing that the victim is, to a more than usually greater extent, in their power. The possibility of being able to inflict an injury on a vulnerable victim is sufficient when this happens to fulfil the sadistic impulse. It is, however, this particular impulse which explains the cases of wanton and excessive cruelty which sometimes shock and outrage a nation.

A good illustration of the masochistic involvement with bodily defects is provided once again by Krafft-Ebing, who supplied no detailed analysis of the particular case, but which is sufficient in itself to suggest a very clear explanation of the patient's bizarre addiction.

'X, twenty-eight years old, comes from a seriously afflicted family. He is neurasthenic, complains of a lack of self-confidence and frequent depression with suicidal inclinations, against which he has difficulty in defending himself. At the least untoward event, he says he is quite disconcerted and feels desperate. The patient is an engineer, of strong build, no signs of degeneration. He complains of a curious mania which often causes him to doubt whether he be mentally sane. Since the age of seventeen, he has been exclusively excited in the sexual sense by female deformities, especially women who limp and have twisted feet. The original associative link between his libido and defects of beauty of that kind is quite unkown to the patient.

'Since puberty he has been cursed with this fetishism, which he himself finds painful. A normal woman has but the slightest charm for him, only the one who is twisted and limps, with deformities of the feet. If a woman be possessed of such defect, she exerts on him a strong sexual fascination, no matter whether this woman be lovely or hideous.

'It is exclusively limping females of this kind which hover before him in pollution dreams. Now and then he is unable to resist the impulse to *imitate* a limping woman of the sort. In this situation he gets powerful orgasm and an ejaculation accompanied by a lively sensation of pleasure. The patient affirms that he is very lustful and suffers greatly from the non-fulfilment of his impulse. At the same time it was only at the age of twenty-two that he first tried coitus and has since then only practised it about five times. Albeit potent he found not the least gratification in it. If he had the good fortune to copulate on some occasion with a woman who limped, this would certainly be otherwise. In any case, he can only make the decision to marry a girl with a limp.'

In all probability, the 'forgotten' link between the patient's libido and female physical defects never existed. The clue to this man's aberration is provided by the assessment of his personality which Krafft-Ebing provides at the beginning of the quoted passage. This man obviously felt himself to be inferior and inadequate. When this happens people can compensate for such deficiencies in one of two ways. Either they become bumptious and over-aggressive, or they obtain 'importance' by dramatizing the original lack. Both ways can be said to operate in the case of patient X. By seeking to associate with limping women, he effects a fake contrast, i.e. his own deficiencies appear much smaller when compared with their unmistakable, physical defects. However, it is the masochistic exaggeration of his own failings which would appear to be most strong here. This is especially indicated by his desire to imitate a limping woman. He is thereby identifying himself entirely with another flawed human creature. He is exaggerating and simultaneously enjoying sexually his own worthlessness. The limping woman, therefore, seems to him a less fortunate creature than himself and one who has excitingly suffered more. She is a constant reminder of the world's harshness, which concept sexually excites him. This masochism is further underlined by his transvestite tendencies, upon which Krafft-Ebing later remarks. He increases his identification with the weak, defective female image by dressing as a member of the *weaker* sex.

One very important general point which this case raises is the fact that the man has no deep aversion to intercourse. Indeed, he contemplates marrying and likes to imagine the pleasurable effects of copulating with a suitably disabled woman. Thus Krafft-Ebing's usual dictum about the importance of the attitude to intercourse does not apply here. Very often defect fetishists express themselves sexually via intercourse, but, of course, the partner must always have the relevant injury or disablement. This is because, as we have mentioned, it is seldom possible for the fetishist to have any meaningful or pleasurable sexual contact with the injury or defect itself. The attraction of the impaired part is exclusively psychological or emotive. Very often actual sexual contact is not even desired, but if it is, it invariably takes the normal form. When sexual contact is absent, the fetishist is generally content to masturbate, accompanying this activity with fantasies and images of people who have the desired disability.

In amplification of this point and of the masochistic type of attraction involved in defect fetishism, it is worth referring to the strange case of Albert K who had an extraordinary emotional bond with Elizabeth S. Albert K was thirty-nine and had never married. He seldom stayed in any job for long and seemed to be absolutely incapable of forming any deep or lasting personal relationships. That is until he met Elizabeth S.

'I was out of work at the time. Had no place to go. I was sitting in a little park, a public garden you might say, when I saw this woman on a bench down the path a way. She was in a terrible state. Her face swollen and cut. A black eye. Her lips all puffed up. And her legs were one mass of bruises. She was sitting there crying and helpless. I went up to her. I don't know now how that came to be. Usually I can't go up to people and start chatting. It's not my nature. I always expect them to tell me to push off. But I went up to her. I couldn't resist it, you see. I sat beside her, spoke to her. Looking at her poor bruised face and legs got me all worked up. I had an erection. That doesn't often happen to me. Not like it does to some men.

'Anyway, we got talking and she told me about this man, her husband. It seems he beat her something dreadful. She told me all about it and the more I heard, the more I got worked up. It seemed to do her good, talking. I arranged to meet her again.'

Albert K is, in fact, socially inadequate, unable to make contact with people and fundamentally afraid of doing so.

The necessary courage to enable him to speak to Elizabeth S came from a sense of sexual excitement. And once the contact was made, both compassion and masochistic excitement cemented the very curious relationship. His inadequacies seemed nothing in comparison with Elizabeth S' injuries, thus allowing him, through false contrast, to play the normal masculine role which is usually beyond him. But he also found that her account of her husband's sadism and the visual evidence of its enactment greatly excited him. He in fact identified with Elizabeth S, and imagined himself as the recipient of this cruelty. To Elizabeth S he was, of course, the uninvolved comforter she desired. As Albert K said, they arranged to meet again, and this led to a considerable improvement in his circumstances.

'I wanted to go on seeing her, so I found myself a job and made myself stick to it. I took a little room, nothing much, but it was somewhere warm and private to take her. She could only get away in the afternoons, so I took a night job and I forced myself to hang on to it because I knew that seeing her depended on me having the time and the place.

'The first time she came to my little room, the injuries had cleared up and I felt disappointed. But I got her talking about her husband and she said he'd used a strap on her. "Where are the marks?" said I. After a bit of persuasion she showed me. All down her back and her bottom were raw welts and dried drops of blood. He'd worked her over with a belt. The whole time I was looking, and afterwards, I had an erection, and when she'd gone I lay on my bed and thought about him laying into her with the belt while I brought myself to a climax.'

And this, simply, is the essence of their relationship. Elizabeth S visits him regularly, at least once a week, and displays the injuries her husband has inflicted upon her. She also describes in detail the circumstances of her beatings and her husband's insatiable sexual demands. All this excites Albert K as nothing else in his life has ever done, and after each visit, and between them, he masturbates, re-creating mentally the circumstances of Elizabeth S' punishment. This bizarre relationship has had a considerable stabilizing effect upon him and presumably, although it was not possible to check this, offers comfort and emotional release to Elizabeth S herself. Certainly he makes no sexual demands upon her, although he does closely inspect her injuries. She is, presumably, glad to have someone to talk to about her troubles and is comforted by knowing a gentle, sexually undemanding man.

Like Krafft-Ebing's patient X, Albert K has some transvestite tendencies. He has bought various items of female underwear which resemble those worn by Elizabeth S. Occasionally he likes to dress in these and imagines that her husband is beating her, i.e. him. There are, obviously, overtones of incipient homosexuality in this close identification with Elizabeth S. He is very curious about her husband, and has persuaded her to show him a photograph of him. He was very impressed by the man's 'brutal good looks'. Further investigations revealed that he was, as a child, very frightened of his father who appears to have been something of a tyrant. On two occasions he witnessed his father striking and beating his mother, though he does not recall that this unhappy spectacle excited him at all. He remembers comforting his mother and feeling very close to her at such times. Yet despite this he did not hate his father, although it contributed to his fear of him. He also remembers being very impressed on one occasion when he saw his drunken father's erect penis which was, appar-

ently, extremely large. He associates big genital development with masculine cruelty and the two elements attract
him sexually and masochistically, an attraction which is
apparently fulfilled by his relationship with Elizabeth S.

It sometimes happens that these fetishistic relationships
are free of any masochistic involvement, yet cannot properly be called compassionate. A case came to light some
years ago which illustrates this aspect of the fetishism.
Joseph B's entire life, and particularly the sexual areas of
it, had been concerned with those less fortunate than himself. As a young man, he trained as a male nurse, specializ-
ing in the care of the mentally ill. He was dismissed from
his first post, however, for a series of sexual assaults on
female patients. Subsequently, he led a strange nomadic
life acting as a nurse companion to various disabled and
physically defective men and women. He was nearly
always dismissed from these posts when his sexual involvement in his work became apparent to his employers.
His was, in fact, a fairly unspecified form of fetishism, for
he did not display any strong preference for one particular kind of defect. What was of supreme importance was
that the object of his sexual attentions should be, in some
way, disabled. With a normal healthy woman he was entirely impotent. Over and above this, however, he sought
to establish his power over the patients he was supposed
to care for. He was not a sadist and never indulged in any
overt cruelty towards them. He simply liked to impress
upon the patients, often at great length, that he, being
physically whole, was stronger, less vulnerable than them.
This need manifested itself even with male patients, although he was completely hererosexual and never made
any advances towards the males he was engaged to care
for. But with a complete disregard for the age or beauty of

his female patients, he always tried to seduce them and even to force them to have intercourse with him.

Joseph B suffered from an acute inferiority complex. He was the only child of extremely strong and active parents who made no secret of the fact that they found him a disappointment. He grew up, therefore, constantly in the shadow of others. He believed that he was fundamentally inadequate, that others found him a figure of fun. His impotence was, of course, the strongest manifestation of this sense of failure. As a result, he sought out people who presented no threat. He operated on the principle of false contrast. Only when he was faced with a human being who was demonstrably less able than himself, through the loss or impairment of some limb, for example, could he summon up the necessary confidence to assert himself sexually. In this respect he resembled many child molesters. These latter frequently suffer from a similar sense of fear and social inadequacy which leads them to choose vulnerable children as their sexual partners since they are, by virtue of their age and greater strength, more powerful, better able to deal with any resistance offered by the sexual partner. So it was with Joseph B who saw an amputated leg or withered arm as a symbol of his superiority. But the fact that he could only copulate with such physically defective women qualifies him as a defect fetishist.

From the conventional female point of view, Clara Y had many disadvantages. She was plain, gauche, over-tall and always looked older than her age. She had no success with men whatsoever, and, like so many women in this position, she sought compensation in good works. She was painfully shy with men and shunned their company, until she saw the possibilities presented by Ian H. This unfortunate man was several years younger than her, had lost both

legs below the knee in an accident and was partially para-
lysed above the waist.

'His sheer helplessness excited me. The moment I met
him, I knew that I wanted to devote my life to him. He
was very gentle and kind, as people who have suffered a
great deal invariably are. For the first time in my life I
didn't feel at a disadvantage. The way I looked, my size,
just didn't matter. Compared to Ian I was very fortunate
indeed. I felt instinctively that he wouldn't laugh at me,
or find me physically disgusting.'

At first her impulse was primarily maternal. But she was
by then in her mid-thirties and had experienced years of
sexual frustration. She wanted both someone to care for
and to sleep with, but the maternal and erotic impulses
had become completely confused in her mind. She began
to mother Ian H, but this act of caring for a disabled man
was also deeply erotic.

'I began to get sexually excited just being near him. I
used to look at his stumps under the bedclothes and feel a
strange mixture of desire and sadness. I would become
very wet and palpitating between my legs. One day, I could
stand it no longer. I was in a sort of trance. I pulled the
bedclothes off him. He was wearing a nightshirt. I pulled
it up and began to caress and kiss his poor wounded legs.
I was crying and laughing at the same time. I would have
done anything for him, and I worked my way up his thighs.
He had an enormous penis and under my touch it began
to grow hard. Some devil drove me to kiss it, to take it in
my mouth. I felt as though I was in an ecstatic trance. I
wanted to give myself entirely to him. I straddled him and
gave him my virginity. After that first, wonderful experience, I lay with him whenever I could. I knew it helped
him. I was very strong and I was able to lift him on top of

me and move his poor shattered body so that he could make love to me.'

This macabre relationship was abruptly ended when Ian H made complaints against Clara Y. She was dismissed from her job as an unqualified visitor at the clinic he inhabited, but Clara Y utterly rejects that this had anything to do with Ian H's wish. However, her behaviour now became similar to that of a nymphomaniac, with this difference, that she offered herself to disabled or injured men. She attached herself in one capacity or another to various clinics and homes for the disabled and had sexual relations with as many men as possible. She was, eventually, always discovered and was subsequently referred for treatment herself.

Compassion is, at least on the superficial level, an influential factor in Clara Y's behaviour. She is also compensating for her own physical unattractiveness and shyness by choosing men who are 'worse off' than herself. But underneath these obvious impulses there lies a quasi-religious motivation, a sort of assertion of the true feminine role. Clara Y, when she couples with a disabled man, feels that she is bringing him an almost divine comfort. She is making a sacrifice of herself and her motives are compounded of a desire to compensate them for their losses and to gain her own sexual satisfaction.

Women who place themselves in this sort of position generally do so as a result of some lack in their own personalities. Fundamentally, no matter what her attitude, at the moment of intercourse a woman enjoys the impression of being subjugated to the powerful male. Women like Clara Y, for a variety of reasons, know that this is not going to happen to them in the ordinary way, and so they tend to confirm their own lacks by fixing their intermingled maternal and sexual impulses on disabled men. At the hands of such men it is generally impossible for them to be subjected, yet this fundamental masochism of the female psyche is satisfied by an ecstatic sense of service. They are responsible for the sexual act, manage to convince themselves that they are making some great and noble sacrifice when in fact they are simply indulging themselves. Such complex motives have much in common with certain states of religious ecstasy. The individual gains a curious, essential, pleasure from the feeling and act of subjugating herself, either out of an impulse to worship, or to compensate another person for their losses. Such relationships can, of course, work for the patient's good and many valuable ones have been based on exactly these premises. But when, as in Clara Y's case, they become primarily selfish and compulsive, they are a danger to both parties.

These are, of course, very complex forms of defect fetishism and they deviate in many ways from the normal pattern of the aberration as it generally manifests itself. Let us therefore now look at some of the more straightforward cases. For example, the following case which was recorded by Krafft-Ebing.

'V, thirty years old, a clerk, the child of highly neurotic parents. From the age of seven years, for years on end his playmate was a limping girl of the same age.

'From the age of twelve this at all times nervous and hypersexually constituted lad got into the habit of masturbation, without any question of being misled into it. About this same time he became pubescent and there can be no doubt that V's first sexual excitements in relation to the opposite sex coincided with the sight of the limping girl.

'From now on it was only limping women who awoke

174

his sensualism. His fetish became a lame woman, limping just like his childhood's playmate, with the *left* foot.

'The exclusively heterosexual, and with it, in matters sexual, abnormally thirsty, V endeavoured quite early to get into contact with the opposite sex but was absolutely impotent with women who did not limp. His potency and gratification reached peak when the woman limped with the left foot, but he did have successful intercourse with others who limped with the right. Since as a result of his fetishism it was but rarely that he could have coitus he compensated by masturbation which, however, appeared to him a pitiable substitute and quite repugnant. Owing to his situation sexually, he was often extremely unhappy and near suicide, being kept back from it only by his parents' solicitude.

'He suffered morally most of all because he thought of marriage with a lovable limping woman as the aim of his desires, but he felt that in any such wife it was only the limp and not the soul that he could love, which he regarded as a profanation of marriage and felt to be an insupportable and unworthy existence. He had often on that account contemplated renunciation and castration.'

This case demonstrates two very important points which are closely in line with the majority of other forms of fetishism. Firstly, V's predilection is clearly, if unnaturally, dictated by simple orgasm association, which once again underlines the importance of the circumstances of a child's first conscious sexual experience. Secondly, the case shows how very exclusive the fetish object can be. Only limping women attracted V, and there was a strong and recognizable preference for those who limped with the left foot. To one who is not similarly addicted, it would seem to make no difference at all which foot the woman limped with, but to V it was immensely important simply because all his adult sexual activities were an attempt to re-create his first sexual experience which, we recall, involved a girl who limped with the left foot. Furthermore, Krafft-Ebing clearly pinpoints the difficulties and objections which effect and inhibit the sexual fulfilment of such fetishists and the neuroses to which they unfortunately lead.

Orgasm association is also directly responsible for Donald M's fetishistic involvement with women who have to wear a plaster cast as a result of breaking a leg. He explains:

'I was a very inexperienced youth. I began masturbating at about thirteen, but I had no relations with women until I was much older, nineteen or twenty. I was also sexually ignorant. But when I was sixteen, I was very friendly with a much more sexually extrovert and informed boy of the same age who was always boasting about his sexual exploits. At the time he was going out with a girl who broke her leg in a riding accident and one afternoon we went together to see her. She had a plaster cast up to her knee and had to get around with the aid of a stick. There was no one in the house but her that afternoon and we sat talking with her. My friend was talking about sex, of course, and the girl didn't seem to mind. She had got all her friends and relatives to sign their names on the plaster cast and we both did the same. My friend signed first and from where I was sitting, I could see that he put his free hand up her skirt while he wrote. That excited me very much and I had an erection when I knelt down in front of her to sign my name. I could see right up her skirt to the crotch of her panties and I took as long as I could because the sight of her thighs and panties excited me so much.

'Anyway, after that she asked us to make some tea and I went out to the kitchen with my friend. As soon as we were alone, he told me that he was going to try to have the girl, and that I was to take as long as possible making the tea. That excited me even more and after he had gone back into the room, I tiptoed out and peeked through the door, which he had left partly open. He'd drawn the curtains and was making love to the girl. She had her good leg up on the sofa and the other one was sticking straight out in front of her. He knelt between her legs and I saw them copulate. After a few minutes, I had an orgasm in my pants, and then I returned to the kitchen.'

Because of this strange voyeuristic experience, women with their legs in plaster casts came to exert a powerful erotic influence over Donald M. He began to hang around the out-patients department of the local hospital in order to see women so afflicted. He masturbated more and more, always recalling the scene he had witnessed between his friend and the girl with the broken leg. He did manage to have intercourse with non-injured girls, but not very often and with very little pleasure. Eventually he succeeded in persuading a married woman to have intercourse with him daily while her leg was in plaster, but the moment she was well again and the plaster was removed he lost interest in her. He has occasionally been able to prevail upon a girl to bind one leg in thick bandages to create the impression of injury, and this is fairly successful in satisfying him. It is, however, extremely difficult for him to find ideal partners, especially since the injury he requires is inevitably temporary. He has found a novel substitute with which to alleviate his frustrations, however. He writes long stories about girls with their legs in plaster, exploiting the fact that this immobilizes them to a certain extent and graphically describing how they cannot resist being raped by various men who come into contact with them. These stories, which he uses as masturbation material, display an element of sadism and indicate his fear that a woman will resist his sexual overtures unless she is in this way immobilized. His favourite theme, however, and the one which most frequently occurs in his stories, repeats his first experience. The narrator of his story watches a man or series of men copulate with a girl with a broken leg. This again indicates his fear of women and his hesitation in approaching them.

Sadism stands in a very complex relationship to defect fetishism. For some people it is sufficient to be in intimate contact with a physical defective who unwittingly acts as a sort of permanent reminder of the possibility of sadism. The sadist is, in this instance, sexually excited by the defect, not for any associative reasons or for any particular attractions it may hold for him, but as evidence of some cosmic cruelty which in some mysterious way seems to confirm his sadistic interest. In such cases, he likes to pretend that he is the cause of the defect or injury, will encourage the partner to talk about the pain he or she has experienced. For such people, intercourse itself becomes an act of latent sadism and not a simple means of sexual expression. When performing intercourse he is excited by the knowledge of injury and has the impression that he is adding to the victim's pain. This is, of course, essentially a cerebral form of sadism which is confirmed by the presence of existing injuries or defects.

There are, however, more overt and obvious forms of sadism which have a strong connection with defect fetishism. One such concerns Benjamin U. He was a confirmed sadist who had always taken pleasure in another's pain. His first involuntary orgasm occurred while he was cruelly twisting the arm of a young girl. Sexual excitement was always intimately connected with pain as far as he was concerned, and he was specifically attracted to women with some physical defect, for the reasons we have already discussed. The implied helplessness and increased vulnerability of these women greatly appealed to his sadism. In his early thirties, he began a sexual relationship with a girl who had a withered right arm. This attracted him in the first place, and he took great pleasure in taunting the girl about her defect before he had intercourse with her. She had very little control over this arm, and Benjamin U, like the true sadist he was, would compel the girl to try to masturbate him with the withered arm. When she failed, he beat her and then copulated with her. The inevitable clumsiness to which she was prone as a result of this unfortunate disability was also punished by whippings. The infliction of pain always aroused him, and he confessed to finding even greater pleasure in torturing someone who was already impaired. Whatever punishment he decreed, he always followed it with intercourse. Indeed, it should be understood as a peculiarly nasty form of sexual foreplay.

Benjamin U was seriously unbalanced. He believed that the punishment he meted out to helpless women was just, especially when the girl concerned already had some defect for which he was not responsible. He saw such defects as a visible sign of wrongdoing, a sort of divine punishment for some unspecified sin which gave him the right to provide further chastisement.

Another case is remarkable for the presence of both sadistic and masochistic elements, as well as being dictated by early orgasm association. As an adolescent, Philip A badly gashed his thigh during a game, with the result that he had to have several stitches put in the wound and to attend hospital daily to have it dressed.

'The nurses excited me,' he said. 'I used to have to take off my trousers and sit in just my underpants in a little cubicle. Then the nurse would come and remove the old bandage, clean the wound, and put a new dressing on. The very first day I got an erection from these ministrations. One day, the nurse noticed and she deliberately brushed my erection through my pants as she fixed the bandage. That excited me terribly and I used to masturbate as soon as I got home, imagining myself lying naked on a bed while a sexy young nurse changed my bandage and played with my penis. I used to try to ejaculate over the bandage so that the nurses would notice. I think some of them did, but they never asked me the cause of the stain.'

Now, many years later, Philip A is immensely excited by anyone wearing a bandage. He has a gruesome collection of photographs of people with bandaged heads and bodies which he employs as masturbatory aids. At times he has inflicted small flesh wounds on his own body, just in order to wear a bandage, which greatly excites him. He has also made small cuts on women at various times, because the subsequent sight of their bandaged injuries has so greatly aroused him. He has even learned first aid in order to obtain some close contact with injured people. He has followed people wearing bandages in the street, being sexually aroused the whole time. A bandage which is worn without a wound underneath does not attract him at all. Both his masochistic and his sadistic acts are perpetrated not for themselves but in order to allow him contact with a bandaged person. This strange predilection came to light when he sexually assaulted a youth who had been referred to him to have a pulled thigh muscle bound. The situation had obvious parallels with that of his own youth and he had attempted to arouse the boy in the same way that the nurses had unknowingly aroused him.

The cases we have discussed show the range of defect fetishism and some of the more complex motives which cause people to become so addicted. It is an unusual and uncommon form of fetishism and is the one which most clearly reveals the lacks and inadequacies of the fetishists themselves. To most of us it seems unpardonably callous and disturbing that someone should be sexually aroused and attracted by something that is already regarded as lamentable. However, we should remember that it is common for certain African tribes to deliberately disfigure themselves in order to make themselves more attractive. We have all seen the decorative cuts on the cheeks of some Africans and read of the various means of distending the ear lobes and nostrils in the name of beauty. These processes are always painful and always result in some defect, cf. the one-time Chinese practice of binding a woman's feet. All this only proves, however, that beauty is entirely relative, and that club feet, withered arms, etc., can exert a sexual fascination over certain individuals, just as deliberate distortions of the human body can make a person more attractive if this is the recognized ideal of beauty.

Conclusion

ANY study of fetishism immediately underlines the in-estimable importance of childhood and adolescent experi-ences in the fixing of the sexual focus. Of course, these experiences are influential in any form of aberrant sexual-ity, but they are perhaps most clearly seen in cases of fe-tishism. To recapitulate, what happens is that some unusual circumstance intrudes upon the early orgasm experience or accompanies it in some way which makes it seem to be an integral part of the sexual experience itself. Later it be-comes a necessary part. To the sophisticated adult who has a clearly defined sexual impulse such happenings are diffi-cult to understand. Unless there is some special reason to remember most people forget the overwhelming impact of their first orgasm and in the light of later superior know-ledge it seems to them an easy matter to distinguish be-tween the physical sensations of sexual pleasure and some passive object or garment that may be involved. But a pub-escent child all too frequently lacks any such knowledge and ability. To him the first orgasm experience is a shatter-ing, all-embracing event. He does not seek to, nor is he able to, rationalize what is happening to him. His mind and body are simply diffused with an amazing new pleas-ure, and in retrospect, anything which contributed to that pleasure seems to be a prerequisite.

What we should also bear in mind is that the child does

not trust his own unaided abilities to re-create this pleasure at will. It is so new and so completely unlike anything else he has known that it simply does not seem possible that it is entirely his doing. Furthermore, these experiences are very often either solitary, or involuntary if another person is involved. This often suggests to the overwhelmed mind that this marvellous new sensation is fundamentally and essentially private. This, of course, may not be a bad thing in itself, but it may create difficulties later on when the adolescent or young adult finds that he is inhibited about sharing his sexual expression. He may feel ashamed or simply acutely timid, and when this happens, some object which he has already learned to associate with orgasm pleasure may seem in every way preferable.

At this point, we will digress a little for a moment, to examine the importance of early sexual association to women. As we have seen, and as every research into the field of sexual fetishism always reveals, women are much less susceptible to fetishism than men. One reason for this may be, we would like to suggest, the difference in orgasm experience which results from the differing sexual natures of men and women. A man can masturbate and experience physical sensations which are closely akin to those he experiences in actual intercourse. In other words, masturbation can be a satisfactory substitute for intercourse in the case of the male. But even women who have a marked preference for masturbation (and even these are few in number) agree that there is a considerable difference between a manually induced orgasm and one which results, physically and psychologically, from complete male penetration. For the majority of women, masturbation is an unhappy and, in the final analysis, an unsatisfying substitute. Whether this is because the woman experiences a definable vaginal orgasm or whether it is a psychologically produced impression is a matter of some controversy which need not concern us here. The fact remains that women have (*a*) a stronger impulse towards a shared sexual expression and (*b*) agree for the most part that masturbation is but a pale imitation of the sensations they experienced in coitus. This we would suggest greatly weakens the girl's chances of becoming fetishistically involved via early orgasm experience. In so far as she has any thoughts beyond the immediate sensation of pleasure they are almost certain to take the form of a longing for a human partner. The difference is, then, that the female is aware of achieving only part of her sexual pleasure potential via masturbation, whereas the male can be completely satisfied. In other words, the woman will not automatically regard masturbation as the end of pleasure but will seek a partner to take her to greater heights, while the male will seek to recreate that first delightful experience as completely as possible, which makes him more aware of attendant circumstances or potential fetish objects.

It is not, however, enough today to regard this question of early orgasm association in fetishism as an open and closed book. The tendency is to maintain that the individual associates his sexual pleasure with the object as a result of some early experience and to regard this as a complete explanation of the case. It is, however, only half the story. It is not only a matter of the individual preferring the object to the human partner, for, given a satisfactory subsequent development, there is no reason to assume that the fetishist will not outgrow his fetish object as he does his other toys, that he will not emulate the normal man and eschew masturbation in favour of intercourse. That he demonstrably does not indicates the presence of this other half of the story. In other words, not only does the patient prefer the object, but he fears, or has some aversion to, the proper partner. It is true that he first shows a preference for the object out of ignorance and the false focusing of his sexual impulse but this initial stage is sorely aggravated by his failure to relate satisfactorily to the proper human partner. In a sense we may suggest that the original infatuation is increased by the failure to transfer successfully to the human partner. This may be the result of rejection, of disgust, but it may also be directly attributable to the fetishist himself who 'blames' the partner for her natural inability to reproduce the sensations he expects from, and associates with, the fetish object.

Any study of fetishism, therefore, cannot escape the conclusion that this is primarily an aberration which is concerned with a cerebral sexuality, or 'sex in the head'. Under ideal conditions, the body and the mind work closely together. The physical sensations of foreplay and intercourse are aided and abetted by the interplay of two minds, two personalities. The fetishistic man can easily settle for an object as a physical substitute for the woman, although, as we have pointed out, this is not comparably as easy for women. However, he cannot reproduce that sense of intimate sharing, that mental communication which is sometimes regarded as the essence of successful sexuality. Indeed, he does not want to share himself in this way, perhaps because he is afraid of being made vulnerable through such intimacy. Instead he is receptive to the emotive connotations or 'messages' which the object contains for him. Instead of close intimacy with a particular woman, he has a cerebral intercourse with a diffuse and idealized concept of femininity. It is, of course, this which provides the very basis of his extreme loneliness but it is also what protects him from what he considers to be the dangers of human relationships. In the eyes of the fetishist, then, the object is not passive and meaningless, as it is to us, but a genuine source of thrilling sexual ideas and concepts.

With regard to the differing attitudes of the sexes as revealed by aspects of our previous discussion, we may generalize by saying that the fundamental difference between man and woman is that the former seeks to widen the scope of sexual fulfilment whereas the latter's instinct is always to narrow and particularize. This is why a man is both more susceptible to the erotic overtones of fetish objects and more ready to accept the fetishistic needs, if any, of a woman. Women, on the other hand, naturally fix their sexual impulse not only on men but from preference, in the majority of cases, on one man. Anything which distracts his libido from them is seen, therefore, as a loss of attention, love and sexual attraction. This, as we have attempted to explain in the foregoing pages, is because a woman recognizes that, fundamentally, she is dependent upon the male partner for complete sexual expression and fulfilment. A man, however, knows that he is not and that he is essential in this sense. No matter how much he may prefer to express himself, in the final analysis, with a woman, he is also ready and willing to find sexual excitement elsewhere and by other means.

In short, everything about fetishism indicates some fundamental lack on the part of the fetishist. It may be expressed by saying that the fetishist settles for less because he feels himself unable to cope with, or perhaps even to merit, the normal sexual involvement. Fetishism is invariably a form of compensation. It is very rare indeed to find a satisfied and content fetishist, one who knows what he is missing and is prepared to accept the substitute happily. He fixes upon the fetish for whatever reason and then, when it is much too late, discovers that his dependence upon it is total. And, of course, this inevitable, ensuing feeling of frustration is exacerbated by society's condemnation of his behaviour and activities. Yet in comparison with other sexual aberrants the fetishist very seldom indulges in anti-social activities. When he does, these are invariably the result of pressure and frustration, and cause only a minor nuisance. From the humanist point of view it seems particularly unfeeling for society to take such a condemnatory view of the fetishist when society itself is invariably responsible for his condition in the first place.

In the long term, fetishism is directly attributable to the equivocal attitude of society towards sex and its natural expression. If society had not, as we have said, decreed that modesty and bodily decoration were preferable to a natural nudity, then the most common fetish objects would be unknown. Society as a whole has certainly done much to redirect the sexual focus, for not only has it provided ready substitutes, but it has consistently created a need for these by blocking the natural means of expression. But fetishists, and many other deviants, are shaped also by society's assumption about what is the only acceptable means of sexual expression. Society has consistently limited the available areas of sexual expression and each time that it has forbidden it has unwittingly provided the timid and the frustrated with an attractive alternative. In general, feitshists are the victims of social assumptions about sexual relationships. Society assumes that a man will be drawn to a woman and insists that he observe certain behavioural codes in achieving sexual unity with that partner. To the majority, nothing could be easier or more desirable, but for a considerable minority of men this seems to be an impossible and even repugnant task. They feel the pressure of society to make them behave in certain accepted ways and this pressure becomes an intolerable and inhibiting burden. As a result they are driven back on substitutes, forced into a fantasy world of vague feelings and condemned activities which preclude their ever entering the normal world of sexual fulfilment.

In other words we should never lose sight of the fact that fetishism is only one of many sexual aberrations which must be primarily regarded as a social disease. It is an attempt to find fulfilment without the strictures of society. It is an alternative to that which is apparently closed to the fetishist. Furthermore, we should remember that it is, in itself, a symptom of social inadequacy. This inadequacy may manifest itself in several areas of life but it is in the sexual field that it is most keenly felt and most immediately obvious. We tend to forget that a fetishist never consciously chooses. He *needs* the object, and to need implies not only a lack of choice but also a definable gap or hollow which must be filled if the individual is going to achieve any degree of satisfaction. On the simplest level he needs the fetish object to arouse him, to make him capable of sexual performance, and on the most complex he requires it to satisfy an emotional inadequacy, to give him the semblance, the symbolism, of interacting with his fellows.